Rants and Raves for Steve Burt

Odd Lot: Stories to Chill the Heart is a collection of wonderfully chilling tales that will leave you howling with pleasure. Readers of all ages will enjoy this collection. Pack it in your kids' footlocker when they head to camp, but be sure to read it first! Highly recommended.
— J.L. COMEAU, Horrow Writer & Editor, www.countgore.com

Even Odder: More Stories to Chill the Heart will do what the title infers and even more. These creepy tales will have you shaking in your shoes as you read stories about banshees, vampires, wendigos and other assorted and unknown creatures. Five Stars.
— ELYSE THIBODEAU, *The Examiner*
  (Southeast Texas Entertainment

Personally, scary stories don't scare me, but some of these did. Steve Burt really wrote *Even Odder* with a lot of suspense. He described the setting and the characters so well that the reader could feel like you were in it. I would recommend this for boys and girls because it is a good book to read to and with your family. People who like scary stories would like this book. In my opinion it was a ten out of ten.
— REVIEW BY STEVE, A student at Hellen Keller Middle
  School, Easton, CT (posted on school's web site)

The average young adult reader who likes creepy stuff will probably enjoy these tales very much; I know I would have at that age. By all means buy *Even Odder* for the young person on your list who likes spooky tales.
— REVIEW BY ROB GRANO, *All Hallows 34*, Magazine of the
  Ghost Story Society

Awards

NOMINEE/FINALIST, **Bram Stoker Award for Young Readers**, Horror Writers Association

SILVER MEDAL, **Benjamin Franklin Award Best Mystery/Suspense Book** Publishers Marketing Association

FINALIST, **Best Juvenile/Young Adult Fiction** *ForeWord Magazine* Book of the Year Awards

SOLE HONORABLE MENTION, **Best Horror** *ForeWord Magazine* Book of the Year Awards

RUNNER-UP, **Best Genre Fiction**, *Writer's Digest* 10th International Self-Published Book Awards

RUNNER-UP, **Best Inspirational,** *Writer's Digest* 10th International Self-Published Book Awards

FINALIST, **Best Adult Audio Fiction** *ForeWord Magazine* Book of the Year Awards

3 **Ray Bradbury Creative Writing Awards**

7 HONORABLE MENTIONS **Year's Best Fantasy & Horror**

Oddest Yet

Also by Steve Burt

Wicked Odd
Still More Stories to Chill the Heart
Burt Creations 2005

Even Odder
More Stories to Chill the Heart
Burt Creations 2003

Odd Lot
Stories to Chill the Heart
Burt Creations 2001

A Christmas Dozen
Christmas Stories to Warm the Heart
Burt Creations 2000 (paperback)
2001 (audiobook) 2002 (hardcover)

The Little Church That Could
Raising Small Church Esteem
Judson Press 2000

Unk's Fiddle
Stories to Touch the Heart
Steven E. Burt 1995 (hardcover)
Burt Creations 2001 (paperback)

What Do You Say to a Burning Bush?
Sermons for the Season After Pentecost
CSS Publishing 1995

My Lord, He's Loose in the World!
Meditations on the Meaning of Easter
Brentwood Christian Press 1994

Raising Small Church Esteem
with Hazel Roper
Alban Institute 1992

Christmas Special Delivery
Stories and Meditations for Christmas
Fairway Press 1991

Fingerprints on the Chalice
Contemporary Communion Meditations
CSS Publishing 1990

Activating Leadership in the Small Church
Clergy and Laity Working Together
Judson Press 1988

Oddest Yet

Even More Stories to Chill the Heart

STEVE BURT

Illustrations by
Jessica Hagerman

Burt
Creations

Norwich, CT

Oddest Yet
Even More Stories to Chill the Heart

FIRST EDITION
Copyright © 2004 by Steven E. Burt

Second Printing 2005

ISBN 10   0-9741407-1-6
ISBN 13   978-0-9741407-1-1

Printed in USA

Inquiries should be addressed to:

Burt Creations

Steve Burt
29 Arnold Place
Norwich, CT 06360

T 866-693-6936
F 860-889-4068
www.burtcreations.com

Illustrations by Jessica Hagerman
Text Design by Dotti Albertine

CONTENTS

About the Author

Little Stevie Burt grew up in the farming and fishing village of Greenport, New York, on Long Island's northeastern tip. He and his cousins Chuck and Spider and their friend Ramon dug tunnels, built tree houses, and ran away from home a few times. Stevie even saved a boy caught in an undertow once (though they both nearly drowned).

The four boys leap-frogged across the rooftops of village stores, explored the village's underground storm drain system, and clubbed hordes of marauding rats at the local dump. Yes, little Stevie Burt had adventures during the day, and when he went to sleep at night they became weirder adventures. Now that he's an adult (a 6'5" Reverend Doctor Steve Burt), all that weirdness comes out in the stories kids and adults love. He shares them every year on dozens of radio stations across the country in the weeks before Halloween.

Steve Burt has been called a master storyteller. He's also a popular inspirational speaker and a multi-award-winning author. He was a Nominee for the Bram Stoker Award for Young Readers (eventually losing out to Harry Potter) and has won the Ray Bradbury Award, the Benjamin Franklin Award (silver) for Best Mystery Suspense Book, *The Storyteller Magazine* Readers' Choice Award, and countless others. Much of his time is spent in classrooms (maybe more than when he was a kid) sharing his weird tales and scary stories during School Author Visits. He also offers writing classes for kids and workshops for teachers.

In November and December the ordained minister and former seminary professor shifts gears to become "New England's Christmas Story Pastor." He reads his heart-warming Christmas stories in churches, senior centers, civic groups, and on radio stations across the country. His book, *A Christmas Dozen: Christmas Stories to Warm the Heart*, was an AudioBook of the Year Finalist and a runner-up for *Writer's Digest's* Best Inspirational Book.

When he's not teaching or performing or working part-time as a church pastor, Steve lets his mind drift back to his adventure-filled childhood, then squeezes out a few more new tales for the rest of us to enjoy. Lucky for us that little Stevie Burt had such a weird and exciting childhood.

Thanks to

…Jessica Hagerman for the great cover art (again) and illustrations.

…Dotti Albertine at Albertine Book Design for taking my basic ideas and transforming them into fantastic front and back covers, also for the lovely interior design.

…Laren Bright for his thoughtful and passionate copywriting.

…Ellen Reid, the top Book Shepherd in the business, who has been my ramrod and organizer since the beginning. If anyone can make a silk purse out of a sow's ear, it's Ellen the optimist, Ellen the visionary.

…Jo Ann Burt, my wife, who supports my artistic efforts emotionally and by keeping her day job.

…Wendy Burt, my daughter, who is not only a professional editor and writer herself, but is somehow able to remain dispassionate when serving as First Reader and later as Final Editor for her Dad's work. Her tender ruthlessness makes the works so much better.

…The Horror Writers Association for its extravagant gesture of support in voting this book's predecessor, *Even Odder,* one of five finalists for the **Bram Stoker Award for Young Readers**. Even when J.K. Rowling's fifth Harry Potter novel was announced as the category winner, I still felt like a winner just to be in such esteemed company.

About the Artist

JESSICA E. HAGERMAN is a freelance illustrator who works primarily in pen and ink. She lives in Massachusetts with her cat and dog. Jessie did the cover and illustrations for *Odd Lot* (which won three awards) and *Even Odder* (which won two). In addition to illustrating CD jackets, books, and occasional medical articles, Jessie uses her degree in Art Therapy to work with children at the Shriners Children's Hospital in Springfield, Massachusetts. She also plays guitar and sings, and is co-proprietor of Peaceful Products.

About the Stories

"Bad Day" was written for a 24-hour short-story competition in 2003.

"Shadow Meadow" was dictated out of thin air into a mini-cassette in March 2003 while walking the dog through a Revolutionary War cemetery in Norwich, Connecticut. The daily storytelling-while-walking-an-hour experiment of February-March 2003 was an attempt to break through writer's block by shifting from writer mode to storyteller mode. It is detailed in the Introduction to *Even Odder: More Stories to Chill the Heart* (Bram Stoker Award nominee), which was made up of 15 stories from the experiment.

"Storming Stephen King's (Summer 1998)" pays homage to Stephen King's "The Body" and its movie version, *Stand By Me*. By an odd coincidence, fright writers Steve Burt and Stephen King were neighbors in Bangor, Maine 1980-83, where both ordered the 99-cent breakfast special at the Fairmount Restaurant most days. Their daughters attended the same junior high school. Burt says it was fascinating to watch a blacksmith construct by hand King's unique wrought-iron-spears fence with its giant-spider gates and vampire-bat guardians on the gateposts.

"The French Acre" (novella) is a Devaney and Hoag paranormal mystery. *Valley News* reporter Hoag and his retired-history-teacher/amateur-photographer father-in-law Devaney were first introduced in "The Witness Tree" (short story) in the collection *Odd Lot: Stories to Chill the Heart*. The duo will appear in another novella, "The Chambers Crypt," when *Wicked Odd: Still More Stories to Chill the Heart* is published in late 2004 or early 2005.

"The Power of the Pen" was dictated in February 2003 as part of the storytelling experiment.

"The Praying Man" isn't about adventure or horror or the supernatural, it's about honoring the mystery and sacredness of death. It earned an Honorable Mention in the 2002 Ray Bradbury Creative Writing Awards Competition and appeared briefly on the

Waukegan Public Library web site in Bradbury's hometown of Waukegan, Illinois. This is its first print-on-paper appearance.

"The Swimmer" was dictated in March 2003 as part of the story-telling experiment.

"Too Deep" was dictated in March 2003 as part of the storytelling experiment.

"Uncle Bando's Chimes" is about bullying and uses stronger language than most Steve Burt stories. But it's hard to imagine members of a terrorizing subway gang using language like "Heck!" and "Darn!" and "Gosh!" The story first appeared in *Heliocentric Net* (Spring 1995) and was widely reprinted in other magazines. It earned an Honorable Mention in the prestigious anthology, *Year's Best Fantasy and Horror*.

Introduction

Why do I write weird tales and adventure stories for young readers?

This question never comes up during school author visits. The kids are just glad somebody does write especially for them. It comes up often with adult audiences, and I'm glad it's been asked. (By the way, I also write award-winning stories and books for adults.)

I write for young readers because it takes me back in time to when there was boundless adventure and mystery in my life. My pre-teen friends and I were building tree houses with rope-walks, swinging on tree vines over leech-infested swamps, and digging secret tunnels to underground forts. In those years we had Saturday-night ice-skating parties at the cemetery pond, explored the village's storm-drain system beneath the streets, and hefted pipes to bash a marauding swarm of dump rats. It was perhaps my favorite age.

Even today I love books, stories, and movies with pre-teen protagonists: Harry Potter with schoolmates Ron and Hermione, Tom Sawyer and Huckleberry Finn, the young frontier heroes in William O. Steele's *Buffalo Knife* and *Wilderness Journey* (books recently reissued), Frodo and company in *The Lord of the Rings*, the Robinson-Crusoe-like boy-hero in Gary Paulsen's *Hatchet*, Gordie Lachance and Chris Chambers in *Stand By Me* (Rob Reiner's excellent film version of Stephen King's "The Body"), and the boys in *Something Wicked This Way Comes* (a film based on Ray Bradbury's short story about Mr. Dark's evil carnival coming to town).

I'm not saying I'm not happy as an adult, because I'm very happy (especially when writing adventure stories and weird tales for young readers). But my mind and heart are most alive, most energized, when I'm magically teleported back to that age. I loved those early years of adventure and mystery, and I miss them still. That's why I write stories for young readers.

TOO DEEP

I'M NOT SURE how old we were when we started building underground forts—me, my cousins Chuck and Spider, and our friend Ramon—third or fourth grade maybe. But I know when we quit: the summer before sixth grade. That was the year we dug too deep.

The concept was simple. Instead of trying to carve out an actual cave underground, we dug a huge hole in the corner of a potato field with a half dozen trenches leading away from it in different directions. Once the hole and the open trenches were dug like extra long graves, we simply covered everything with boards and plywood, then piled three or four inches of dirt on to conceal the digs. That year we even replanted some of the potato seedlings over the top for camouflage and installed secret trap doors at the far end of each tunnel.

We furnished the fort—actually, the big central cavity was dubbed the Main Room—with orange-crate tables we could put our soda bottles on and empty potato sacks we could recline on. In the beginning we navigated the tunnels with flashlights, but after we learned our way we saved batteries by simply feeling our way in and out on our hands and knees. The candles we saved for lighting the Main Room. Chuck and I "borrowed" two kerosene lanterns from our uncle's barn, but we didn't dare use them after Spider said kerosene fumes were dangerous in closed-in spaces.

Still, the kerosene lanterns looked cool on the tables, so we left them there.

Everything was sunny and glorious that summer. When we weren't at the beach baking in the sun, we were enjoying the coolness of our underground bunker where we didn't have to answer to anybody. We had no one to fear and enjoyed a world of our own making. Having seen many movies about World War II, it wasn't hard to imagine ourselves as infantrymen in foxholes and pillboxes, fighting in defense of freedom.

It was Ramon who came up with the idea of digging deeper. In late July with the potato harvest just two weeks off, the four of us were lounging around the Main Room talking about the fort's imminent collapse. A tractor had crashed through the year before and would no doubt crash through again unless we made some adjustments.

"Maybe extra timbers for the roof?" Chuck said. "I saw some old railroad ties behind the barn."

"Extra shoring is a good idea," Ramon said. "But what about going the opposite way, too? How about digging deeper?"

"What do you mean—deeper?" Spider's eyes widened with interest.

"I mean tunneling *down* instead of sideways all the time," Ramon said. "Let's make something more permanent. We could tunnel *beneath* this room and create a real cave, so that if everything else collapsed, the true cave would be too far down to be wrecked."

"We could go up and down a ladder like Tom Sawyer and Huck Finn in the Injun Joe story," Spider said. "We could have a really cool secret cave."

"Are you sure we wouldn't hit water?" Chuck asked, teasing a tiny earthworm that had burrowed in through a wall.

"Nah," Ramon said. "I'm sure the water table's pretty far down here. And if we hit it, no big deal, we stop. Right?"

Even if Ramon didn't know a thing about the water table, he was right about one thing. Digging a tunnel downward—a shaft—and then a large cavern off it, would be an interesting challenge. And if we struck water, that too would be interesting. How could we lose? We laid into the task right then.

It was awkward going at first because it wasn't like our original fort-and-tunnels system. Now we had to work in the cramped quarters of the Main Room, digging straight downward, bringing up buckets full of dirt and lugging them out through the tunnels before we could dump them. The work was exhausting, and we all slept like logs at night. In two days we completed a four-foot by four-foot vertical tunnel descending eight feet. We called it the Shaft.

At the bottom we carved out a new, even deeper big room. It started slowly but grew quickly as the space widened, and by week's end we had an eight-by-eight-foot room that was shored up by timbers supporting a plywood ceiling—just in case. We called the room the Cave. Its floor was nearly twenty-five feet below ground level.

That's when we should have stopped. But instead we decided to probe deeper, adding a sloping tunnel off the Cave's far end. Two days later we had scoured out a fifteen-foot-long tunnel, four-feet high by three-feet wide, with timber-supported plywood above. It looked like a genuine coal miner's tunnel and sloped downward at a fairly steep incline.

On Friday we started off with a meeting in the Main Room. Ramon lay on his potato sack petting Oreo, his Boston terrier who followed us everywhere. Oreo practically belonged to all of us, and had been the runt pup from our terrier Frisky Girl's litter.

"The tractors start Monday, Tuesday at the latest, from what I hear," Chuck said. "So we've only got today, tomorrow, and Sunday. Can't count on Monday." With no discussion, we headed to the Shaft to continue digging the sloping tunnel that Spider said would take us either to hell or China, whichever came first.

We hadn't been at it more than half an hour when my round-nosed shovel broke through into another tunnel—except it wasn't our tunnel. Chuck shone a flashlight in. The new tunnel, a perfectly round one, was about three feet in diameter and cut across ours on a slant. It had no boards and no shoring, apparently didn't need any.

"You think kids from another neighborhood dug it?" Spider said.

"Don't know," Ramon said. "And who cares? This'll make things a lot easier for us. Now all we've got to do is square it off and shore it up as we go. Most of the digging's done."

"Who would have dug down this far?" I said.

"And who digs round tunnels?" Chuck scratched his head. "The walls are perfectly smooth, no signs of shovel marks."

Oreo stuck his pudgy snout through the opening and sniffed.

"Maybe we should do a little reconnaissance first," Spider said. "Explore it. Pair off in teams? One team take the up slope, the other team take the down slope?"

Oreo backed out and sneezed, shaking his little doggy head. Then he sneezed again.

"Where do you suppose it goes?" I said.

Chuck shrugged. "Eventually, up to ground level, I suppose."

"And the downhill end?" Spider said.

Nobody answered.

"Maybe it's like an underground storm drain system," Ramon said. "There could be branches off this one."

"Except there's no evidence of water running through this tunnel," Spider said. He shone his light in and wiped a hand across the hard-packed dirt to show us it was dry. "Oh, yuck," he said, pulling back his hand and showing us.

"Looks like dog drool," Ramon said.

"Oreo just sneezed there," Chuck said.

Spider wiped his hand on his pants leg. "No, it's more than that. It feels like snail slime. Or like the path behind a slug." He shone his flashlight in. "I think the tunnel walls are coated with it. I'll be back in five. Just got to run my hands under a garden hose. Yuck."

"Hope it's not radioactive," Ramon said loudly as Spider disappeared up the ladder, and we all chuckled.

"So funny, I forgot to laugh," we heard Spider say before his voice and he disappeared into the darkness of the exit tunnel.

We talked about what we should do next. Ramon suggested getting two stray cats and sending one into the down tunnel, the other into the up tunnel.

"Sure. We could tie strings onto their tails in case we had to pull them back out," Chuck said.

"You're looking more like a cat all the time, Chuck," Ramon said.

We stood in the silence a moment. Oreo gave a low, throaty growl, so Ramon stroked his head and scratched him behind the ears.

"What are we going to do when Spider gets back?" Chuck said.

"We're not seriously going in there, are we?" I said, my heart skipping a few beats at the thought of it. The air felt suddenly thick and hard to breathe.

But there was no time for Chuck or Ramon to answer. From the strange tunnel came a loud sucking sound, like a plunger trying to clear a toilet.

We turned our flashlights on the hole and listened.

"What was that?" Chuck whispered. The sucking noise came from the downhill end and didn't sound all that far off. I took a deep breath, trying to quell the rising fear in the pit of my stomach.

"Whatever it is," Ramon said, leaning into the tunnel to listen, "It's coming in our direction." The sucking sounds came closer together, as if whatever was in the tunnel was picking up speed, climbing the grade faster.

Oreo barked at the break we had made into the round tunnel.

"Let's get out of here," Chuck said, turning and starting up our sloping Tunnel to the Cave. "Fast."

That's when the high-pitched sound kicked in— EEEE, EEEEE, EEEEEE—as if we had set off an alarm. We put our hands over our ears. The blood froze in my veins and I felt the hairs on my forearms stand straight up.

Oreo stood squared-off in front of the break, yapping furiously.

"Let's wall it back up," Ramon shouted, having a hard time making himself heard over the sucking, the EEEing, and Oreo's barking. "We'll put this plywood over the hole," he told me. "Chuck, prop some timbers against it. Maybe it'll go past the patch."

"Or the patch will at least slow it down," Chuck shouted.

I wondered what this "IT" we were talking about could be.

We worked quickly, tearing down the ceiling and the shoring we had put in place earlier, jamming it into place as a makeshift patch. The construction materials muffled the sucking and EEEing slightly, but we could hear that something had almost reached the breach in its tunnel.

Oreo stopped barking. The EEEing and the sucking in the tunnel stopped. We stood stock still, eyes and flashlights on the patch, listening, hardly breathing. A full ten seconds passed.

Crunch! The plywood and timber patch cracked as something heavy bumped against it. Another bump and I saw that the end of one of our 2"x4" braces was now jammed six inches or more into the floor of the Tunnel. What had the strength to force a 2"x4" into the ground that way?

We backed away from the patch.

"It wants to get out," Chuck said. "It's like a train looking for a side track."

Oreo began to bark again and the EEEing and sucking resumed. We could hear wood splintering as it gave way to a strong, steady pressure from beyond.

"Nothing we've got is going to stop it," Chuck yelled, flashlight shaking. "It wants out. It wants to use our tunnel to come up."

More wood splintered and the patch shifted further in our direction as if pushed by the blade of a bulldozer.

"Let's go," Chuck yelled, pulling my arm.

Ramon scooped Oreo up in his arms and we scrambled up the sloping Tunnel to the Cave. Chuck mounted the ladder first and was halfway up when I started. The crunch of wood ceased in the Tunnel behind us. The thing was no longer pushing the patch but had to be squeezing past it.

"Ramon, when I get partway up, hand me Oreo and I'll pass him up to Chuck."

"What's up, you guys?" a voice said from above. I looked up and saw Spider pulling Chuck up into the Main Room. It sure felt good to see him back.

"Pile dirt and anything else you can find at the top of the Shaft," I yelled. "As soon as we're up, dump it all and plug the Shaft!"

The sucking grew closer, the EEEing louder.

"Oh, my God!" Ramon screamed, his flashlight illuminating our Tunnel. "Look at it!"

I backtracked a step down and flashed my light where his was. Oozing from the Tunnel into the Cave was a huge red-gray bloodworm, circular mouth in its slimy head opening and closing like the pupil of a huge fat eye that was continuously dilating and retracting. I stared down its throat and, as I did, something my mother once told me ran through my brain—earthworms eat dirt, in one end and out the other. To this day I have no idea why that thought crossed my mind then. This mutant worm from who-knew-where had escaped the bonds of its three-foot-wide tunnel and was expanding as it suctioned its way along in our wider, higher Tunnel. It was like a liquid, expanding to fill the size and shape of the container. The slime that Spider had scraped from the tunnel wall must have greased the way for the thing's forward movement. And now it was about to reach the Cave, where it would have room to expand even more.

"Get back up the ladder!" Ramon shouted. "And take Oreo!" He held the terrier by its neck like Perseus holding Medusa's head. "Take him!"

I hooked my arm around the ladder rung so I could still handle the flashlight with the same hand, then reached for the dog. The sucking noises grew closer together like a pregnant mother's contractions. It was preparing to move again, and something told me it was bunching up like a Slinky toy gathering its coils, readying itself for a major push forward. What drove it? Sound? Smell? Vibration? Hunger? Anger at us for invading its tunnel? Whatever motivated it, the monstrous, ever-expanding bloodworm was bulldozing its way through our maze toward the surface. And Ramon was next in its path.

"I've got him," I said, grabbing Oreo.

But before I could turn to hand the dog up the ladder, the thing's huge head shot out of our Tunnel—not striking like a cobra, but unfolding the way an accordion does. It advanced halfway across the Cave and seemed to be drawing the latter part of its body along behind it, allowing it to catch up. But now that it was in the middle of the Cave, the sucking sound was more hissy, emptier. With no walls or ceiling to attach its suckers to, with only the floor for traction, forward movement wasn't so easy.

Ramon must have realized it, too. As I shone my light on it, Ramon grabbed a shovel and ran at it.

"What are you doing?" I screamed.

In a flash Ramon was yelling obscenities as he hacked and chopped at the bloodworm's gaping mouth. Again and again he plunged the shovel's sharp, round tip into the thing's blubbery flesh. The EEEing came from the center of its throat, from deep inside, and rose to a fever pitch. A dozen more frenzied jabs with the shovel and the sound ceased.

The Cave was silent.

Ramon stabbed at it one more time, burying the shovel so deep in the inside of the bloodworm's cheek that he couldn't pull it back out. He pulled with all his might, but it was like rubber boots mired deep in mud flats. All I could hear was the sucking sound of his stuck shovel. The thing's reddish skin quickly grew ashen, then a darker gray.

Ramon, panting with exertion, turned and grinned up at us. As he did, Oreo sprang from my arm and landed at the bottom of the ladder. I expected him to run to Ramon, but he didn't. Instead, he squared-off at the unmoving worm and barked, yapped incessantly, refusing to retreat from his offensive posture.

"It's okay, boy," Ramon said soothingly, reaching down for the dog.

The shovel handle moved.

"Ramon!" I yelled.

The massive head jerked forward, as if in a spasm, the dead, gray cheek-flesh falling aside as new reddish-pink flesh poked through from inside. It was like a baby being born. The bloodworm was shedding its dead front layer so it could make its way forward through itself. It was as if it had used its own body as a cocoon, and now a new, round, red, glistening-wet head was pushing out, dilating its mouth muscles, opening and closing as it pressed forward.

Ramon backed toward the ladder, looking frantically for another shovel. But there was none, no weapon, only a couple of boards. He threw those, but they simply disappeared into the new worm's gaping maw, swallowed whole.

"Adios, boys!" Ramon yelled, putting a hand on the ladder. "Time to vamoose!"

The sucking sound commenced again. The worm was pulling its body behind it, readying for another surge. A quieter EEE sound started. I was sure it would grow louder as the thing rejuvenated.

"We're coming up!" I yelled to Chuck and Spider.

"Oreo! Come!" Ramon commanded.

But the terrier held his ground, yapping and making menacing movements toward the worm.

"Oreo! Come here!" Ramon took a step back toward the dog. As he did, the bloodworm's new smaller head shot forward from inside the old head, like a tongue darting out from a mouth.

The feisty terrier didn't back off. He barked, snarled, bared his teeth and charged. And then he simply disappeared.

The worm's dilated mouth rolled shut, enclosing Oreo in its wet fleshy cheek-folds.

"Oreo!" Ramon screamed, and then all was quiet. It

stayed that way for ten or fifteen seconds, as if everyone on the battleground was stunned, or reverent.

Then the sucking and the high-pitched EEEing resumed as the worm adjusted slightly, turning, as if taking aim.

We've opened Pandora's Box, I thought. *How do we close it?*

"Come on, Ramon," I said, and after a moment of glaring at the thing, he turned and followed me up. I was scared to death of the thing in the depths below. Ramon, I believe, wasn't. He may have felt sad and guilty and angry, but I don't think he felt scared.

"Throw anything you can find into the Shaft," I said.

"Where's Oreo?" Chuck asked.

Ramon's look told it all, and Chuck let it drop.

We tossed the orange-crate tables and the empty buckets into the Shaft, then started shoveling in any dirt we could scrape up.

"How about these?" Chuck said, holding up the two kerosene lanterns. "Molotov cocktails, anyone?"

We quickly considered the kerosene lanterns, concluding they wouldn't work as incendiaries if simply lighted and tossed. So we gathered up the burlap potato sacks, soaked them in kerosene, and tied each sack in a knot. We stripped off our tee shirts and did the same. Eight Molotov cocktails. Four outgunned GIs in the battle at the pass.

The ladder at the top of the Shaft trembled, shuddered, and made a cracking sound. The bloodworm had reached the Shaft. The ladder crunched and fell away as the wood broke. I didn't know if the thing was battering it or swallowing it.

"It's coming!" Spider said.

"Everybody pick an escape tunnel," I said. "Once we light the cocktails, let them get burning good. Then drop them. There'll be fumes in the air, so get out fast. Ready?"

Four thumbs up.

"Light 'em if you got 'em," Ramon said, and we lit the sacks and the tee shirts.

"Bombs away!" Chuck said, and one after another we dropped the flaming torches.

The high-pitched EEE intensified. Our enemy was in pain, and over the screeching we could no longer hear the sucking. Maybe it wasn't advancing.

The Shaft looked like a beam of light. We could feel the heat immediately, then smelled the burning cloth and kerosene fumes. And the sweet odor of flesh charring.

"Go! Go! Go!" Ramon yelled, coughing. "Everybody out!"

We scooted through our escape tunnels and a minute later emerged from our trap doors into bright daylight.

"Leave the trap doors open," I said. "Fire needs oxygen to burn. And if the thing survives the fire, hopefully it won't like the sunlight."

"Like Dracula," Spider said.

"I'm not waiting around to find out," Chuck said.

We set out at a trot for the small patch of woods on the edge of the potato field. There we sat for an hour, letting the fear and the adrenaline rush recede as we monitored the trap doors. Nothing appeared, so we left and walked home, trying to make up a story to explain Oreo's disappearance.

Ramon figured ignorance was the best tactic, and he pretended he had no idea where Oreo disappeared to. We all knew his heart was breaking, just as ours were at the loss of our mascot and friend. But we had a bond, the four of us.

The next morning we returned to the fort. The

trap doors were still open and intact. No evidence the worm had made its way to the surface, no slime trail leading away from our diggings. But not even Ramon volunteered to go underground and check things out.

"It probably burned to death in the Shaft," Chuck said.

"Or died of smoke inhalation," Spider said.

"Then again, for all we know," Ramon said, "it could have turned itself around in the Cave. Maybe it's gone back to where it came from."

"And where would that be?" I said.

Ramon smiled a weak smile. "Hell or China, I suppose, whichever comes first."

On Monday, three days after our encounter, Ramon came over to tell us he'd gotten a call from the Dog Warden. The man who ran the Cutchogue Dump—more than five miles away—had found Oreo wandering amongst the trash heaps. He was exhausted and disoriented but otherwise okay. The first thing the Warden did was give Oreo a bath, because when the man at the dump had found him the evening before, the poor dog had been caked with a layer of dirt which hardened over a thick sac of slime.

It was like a cocoon, the Dog Warden said, *like a cocoon that almost fully encased his body except for the tip of his nose. It was all the dog could do to breathe. He could barely walk with the weight of all that dirt on him.*

We sold the two salvaged shovels to kids in the neighborhood for $7, begged a ride to the dog pound with the foreman of the potato farm, then put the $7 toward the $10 Ramon needed for Oreo's bail. The Warden promised never to mention Oreo's brief stay.

Monday evening Oreo miraculously appeared on Ramon's back porch. The family was delirious with joy.

TOO DEEP

The next day the potato harvest began. The fort and tunnels caved in, as they had in the past, under the weight of the tractor. At least, that's how it appeared from a distance. Just as well.

I went to bed that night—and for many nights after—thinking not just about the huge, red-gray bloodworm but also about the Town Dump. I wondered what other horrors were festering beneath the mountains of rotting trash. What monsters were being nurtured by the Dump's weird mix of juices that leached into the soil below? I couldn't imagine what creatures might be there—breeding, mutating, just waiting to seek their freedom farther afield.

We never dug an underground fort again.

STORMING STEPHEN KING'S[1]
(Summer 1998)

THE FOUR CREW CUT BOYS sat around the camp-fire, toasting marshmallows and smoking cigarettes as the caper took shape.

"I'll be the fat kid," said the round-faced boy with raisin eyes. As if there was ever any question he'd be anybody else. He'd always be chunky Vern Tessio.

"Yeah, yeah, we know. And I'm Teddy Duchamp," mocked the kid with the mangled ear and the dog tag

[1] In case there's someone alive who isn't familiar with horrormeister Stephen King, his writings, and the accident that almost killed him, here's a little background. King's novella "The Body" was made into the hit movie *Stand By Me* by director Rob Reiner. The story is told in retrospect by an adult Gordie Lachance (Richard Dreyfuss in the movie) who has just read of the stabbing death of his childhood best friend, Chris Chambers (River Phoenix in the movie). The story that unfolds is about four pre-teen boys in the 1950s (Gordie Lachance, Chris Chambers, Teddy Duchamp, Vern Tessio) who learn by accident that a boy their age has been killed by a train. (Young Gordie's older brother Denny, whom he idolized, had also recently died.) Having never seen a dead body, the four boys take an overnight camping trip to find the body. Along the way fumble-fingered Vern drops his new comb off a trestle while he and Gordie are narrowly escaping a train; Gordie is affirmed as a storyteller/writer; and Gordie (played by a young Will Wheaton) faces down the evil Ace Merrill (played by young adult Kiefer Sutherland). The movie came out in 1986. King continued to write books and became the world's most widely read horror writer. Then in the summer of 1999 fans were stunned by the news that a van had struck Stephen King as he was out walking beside a road near his summer house in western Maine. He barely survived, lives in pain, and is still not the same old Steve King. This story takes place the summer before King's accident.

hanging from a beaded chain on his neck. He pointed at the other two. "And he's Chris Chambers. And this little wiener"—he grabbed the frail boy in a headlock and gave him a noogie with the knuckles of his free hand—"is Gordie Lachance."

"Cut it out, Teddy," the frail kid yelled, pulling free of the headlock. "You morphodite!"

It was always the same. They never switched roles.

"But this time the adventure will be different," said the chunky kid.

"Yeah," said Teddy, leaping to his feet and pretending to spray the bushes with a machine gun. "This time we're assaulting the Eagle's Nest, Hitler's vacation hidey-hole." He used his teeth to pull the pin of an imaginary hand grenade, tossed it, and mouthed the sound of an explosion.

"Got news for you, Teddy," said the trim, muscular kid who was Chris Chambers. "It's not the Eagle's Nest. And it's not Omaha Beach, not D-Day. No guns, no grenades, no bayonets. So relax, Teddy. This is different." He paused and lowered his voice for emphasis. "This is Stephen King's place." The other three sat spellbound, captured by Chris's words. *This is Stephen King's place.*

Words tumbled out of Vern's mouth first. "It's that reddish mansion up by the peak of West Broadway, the one with the iron-spear fence and giant spiders in the gates and vampire bats above them. It's really, really spooky. Sincerely."

"And just how do you know, Vern-o?" Teddy said. "You've never been there."

"I saw it on TV," Vern said. "On the news." Vern was always eager to share information in the hopes it would raise his status with his friends. Vern was also the fraidy cat of the group. Big talk, little action.

"Vern's right," Chris said. "It does look spooky. I saw it on TV, too."

"I read in *Parade Magazine* it's got 25 rooms," Gordie said, lying sideways to the campfire now, head propped on his elbow. "With an indoor swimming pool."

"Wow! That's boss!" Vern exclaimed. "So boss!"

Teddy tugged on his scarred ear and said, "Really? A swimming pool! How cool is that?"

"All right. Now wait. This isn't about the house or the swimming pool," Chris said. "This, this is about a quest, a quest for the Holy Grail."

"Awesome," Teddy said. "The Holy Grail! Right on!" But after a moment, he said, "What's the Holy Grail?"

"It's a figure of speech, Teddy," Gordie said, shaking his head. "When something is referred to as a Holy Grail, the original being the cup Jesus used at the Last Supper—which, by the way, has never been found—it means it's a valuable prize that's always been unattainable."

Teddy nodded as if he actually understood for once. "So this Holy Grail then—not that lost cup, but this one we're after—is what?"

"Stephen King's journal," Vern said.

"Yeah, his writer's journal," Chris said. "That's the real prize."

After a few seconds Teddy said, "Okay, call me stupid, but I don't get it. Storming the house, I understand. And you guys know me, I'm all for adventure. But breaking in and stealing a guy's book, I don't get it." He took a drag on his cigarette, inhaled—something only he and Chris did—and exhaled.

"This isn't just any old book," Chris said. "*It's Stephen King's writer's journal*. This guy's the richest, most famous horror writer in the world. His journal is where he writes down his story ideas."

"And how do we know that?" Teddy said. "How do we know he doesn't just think up the ideas when it's time to write a story?"

"Because," Vern insisted, "he said he writes his great ideas down. I heard some high school kids down at Betts Bookstore talking about it. They said the guy talked about it when he was giving a speech at the Bangor Library. He said it was something every writer should do, keep a writer's journal."

"How can we be sure he's got one?" Teddy said.

"Ask Gordie. He's a writer," Chris said. "You keep one, right, Gord?"

Gordie squirmed and took a puff on his cigarette without inhaling. He tried to casually blow out the smoke a little at a time, in rings, but near the end he coughed and it escaped in a thick cloud. "Sure. It's just common sense. I write stuff down so I don't forget. Sometimes story ideas come in bunches. If I write them and save them, I can go back to them later on. My note-books have both—some stories and some ideas."

"Well," Teddy said, as if everything now made perfect sense, "Count me in. I'm for storming Stephen King's castle."

"It's a house, Teddy," Chris said. "And storming it isn't the point. We just want to get in, get the journal, and get out."

"Yeah, I know," Teddy said. "The Holy Grail." Then his face blanked again. "Okay, so I still don't get it. What's so great about this journal?"

"Think about it, Teddy," Vern said, enjoying the touch of condescension in his voice. "It's worth a fortune."

Teddy blinked and kneaded his scarred earlobe with his thumb and forefinger. "You mean somebody would pay us for it?" he said. "Like spies selling secrets? Or is this like a ransom? Will Stephen King pay us a million dollars to get it back?"

"No, Teddy," Chris said. "Think about it. This guy makes 10 million dollars for every book he writes.

Stealing his journal would be like stealing his brain. We can beat him to the stories and make a fortune."

"Yeah," Vern said. "*We* can be the famous authors."

Teddy and Vern smiled broadly. Then Vern looked perplexed. He turned to Chris and Gordie. "But wouldn't they catch us as soon as they saw our names on the books?"

"Yeah, wouldn't they?" Teddy agreed. "Besides, I'm no writer."

"Me neither," Vern said.

"Ah," Chris Chambers said. "*We're* not. *But Gordie is.* And as for getting caught, we'd use a pen name, like Stephen King used to use Richard Bachman. Only our publisher would know the author's true name, and we'd swear the publisher to secrecy."

"And you three would sponge off my riches," Gordie interrupted, a sly smile curling into his cheek. "Right?"

The three sat quiet a moment.

"What's wrong with that?" Teddy said. "You get to do what you want—write stories. And we get whatever we want—which is maybe nothing. Or Chris might go to college and law school. Vern could buy a bunch of new combs like the one he lost on the trestle when the train almost ran him over. Whatever. That's fair, isn't it? If we storm Stephen King's and get the journal for you, we ought to get something out of it. A four-way split of the profits, right?"

Before anyone could say more, Vern's marshmallow oozed off the end of his stick and plopped into the campfire. "Aw, darn!" he moaned, and everyone roared. Teddy Duchamp reminded Vern what a goober he was and the conversation turned in another direction, including speculation on the outcome of a battle between Mighty Mouse and Superman. Two hours later they were all asleep in their bedrolls.

At 10 a.m. four boys walked up Cedar Street toward 47 West Broadway, hoping they could ad lib a plan to get into the King mansion. Two of them, one chubby with raisin eyes and the other with a scarred ear, walked past Stephen King's place several times. A tall muscular kid and a shorter, frail kid stood on the corner of Cedar and West Broadway, acting like star-struck tourists sizing up the King mansion for souvenir photos. When the street was clear of pedestrians and cars, the first two bolted behind the shrubs of the house next to King's, then scrunched down with a perfect view of the back door. The two on the corner disappeared behind the hedge of the house opposite King's. This vantage point gave them not only a front view of King's house but a sightline to their partners in crime. A simple nod yes or no and they could let Teddy and Vern know if anyone was coming.

At 10:15 a woman opened the back door and stepped out, carrying a white kitchen trash bag.

"It's the cleaning woman," Teddy said. "I never thought about hired help."

"No, Teddy. That's Tabitha King, the guy's wife," Vern said. "I saw her picture on a book jacket down at Bett's. She's a writer, too. Not the scary stuff, though."

The woman deposited the bag in a large green plastic garbage pail and disappeared back inside the house.

"See that, Vern?" Teddy said, chewing a wad of gum.

"See what?"

"She didn't use her key to get back in. It means the back door's unlocked."

"But how does that help us? They'll just lock it when they leave."

"That," Teddy said as he started for the back door, "is why the President himself asked for Private Teddy Duchamp for this mission."

"Be careful, Teddy," Vern whispered.

Ten seconds later Teddy was making himself flat against the red siding of the house, barely a foot from the door, pretending to be an infantryman ready to toss a grenade into an enemy pillbox. Instead of tossing something, though, he pulled the wad of gum from his mouth, opened the door slightly and packed the gum into the tiny opening in the doorframe where the door latch normally clicked into place. He grinned, flashed the thumbs-up to Vern, then sprinted back and leapt into the bushes again, saluting as he squatted down. "Mission accomplished."

Fifteen minutes later the door swung open and out stepped Tabitha King. She slipped her key into the tumbler block, turned it, and walked away without tugging to see if the lock had caught. A minute later she eased the Volvo onto West Broadway and turned toward Union Street.

"Signal Gordie and Chris the coast is clear," Teddy said, standing up.

"Wait, Teddy. What if Stephen King is still in there?"

"Nobody's there, doofus," Teddy said scornfully. "There was only one car in the driveway, and she took it. Besides, why would she lock the door if somebody's home? The guy's off autographing books somewhere."

Vern looked befuddled, but he gave Gordie and Chris a thumbs-up sign and the come-ahead wave. As the other two emerged from behind the hedge, Teddy ran for the door to make sure the trick had worked. It had. He slipped inside. In no time all four boys found themselves in Stephen King's mudroom, preparing to swarm over the house in search of the Holy Grail.

Chris crept forward and found the kitchen. It had a beautiful center island and hanging copper-bottom pots and pans. No butler, no maid, no cook. It looked like the Kings had money but apparently didn't waste it on servants.

"Look at this!" Teddy crowed, making a ghoulish face as he brandished a meat cleaver in one hand and a carving knife in the other. "This must be the torture kitchen, where they dispose of their guests." He cackled with glee.

"Put those back," Chris said sharply.

"Why?" Teddy said. "You worried about fingerprints? We're not on record anywhere."

"No, he's not worried about fingerprints," Gordie cut in. "The point is, we're not here to mess up the guy's house. We're here for the journal, remember? We need to get in and get out."

"Then let's get to it," Chris said. "We split up in pairs. Teddy, you and Vern check the upstairs. Gordie and I will check the downstairs. Don't bother with spare bedrooms or bathrooms, just the master bedroom and anything that looks like a study. If he's got a journal, it'll probably be in a nightstand or near the bed. Look under the bed, too, in case he keeps it where he can grab it to record dreams. Gordie and I may find it down here in an office or something. Check bookshelves, too, and the top shelves of closets, to see if he's got old journals. He may have dozens, like Gordie, or even hundreds, since he's an old geezer now. Got it?"

"Got it!" Teddy and Vern said in unison. Teddy saluted and the boys paired off in different directions.

Chris and Gordie crept through the main level. Something didn't feel right about the place, and it wasn't just the fact that they were there invading it. There was something strange, spooky about it. Mud room, kitchen, laundry room, bathroom, dining room, living room, two closets, den, another closet, family room, another closet, another bathroom, a small office that was obviously hers, a third bathroom, then, at the end of a short hallway, a closed door with a sign: *Quiet. Writer at work.* Chris reached an arm behind him, pressing a hand into Gordie's bony chest to hold him back, just in case. Just in case *what*? In case the door opened and a snarling watchdog charged out? Or a bat swooped down? Crawling spiders? Scuttling scorpions? Maybe a rabid Stephen King himself wielding a machete? Just in case *what*? Chris didn't know. But something might be behind the door, and he needed to protect Gordie. Just in case.

Upstairs, Teddy and Vern searched, Teddy leading, Vern cowering behind. Bedrooms, closets, bathrooms, linen closet, upstairs family room, more closets and bedrooms. They checked a half dozen closets, opened a few dresser drawers. Nothing.

"Ah, let's get out of here," Vern said. "The journal's not up here."

Teddy was staring out the window of the Victorian turret room. "What a great spot for a sniper," Teddy said. "You can see the side and the front of the house. You can cover the whole street from here." He pretended to sight in on a target and made pow-pow sounds.

"Teddy, let's go help Gordie and Chris downstairs," Vern said, his voice shaky now. When Teddy didn't move, Vern backed toward the hallway. "You stay if you want, Teddy, but I'm going."

Teddy frowned. "Fraidy cat Vern." He turned to the window and squeezed off another pretend round, then set his imaginary sniper rifle against the wall and followed Vern to the staircase.

Downstairs, Chris quietly turned the knob and pushed open the door to Stephen King's study. The room was large, dimly lit, and lined with wall-to-wall bookcases. A loveseat, sofa, and an overstuffed chair sat on thick carpeting, grouped around a large library table piled high with magazines, books, and papers.

Two gray filing cabinets stood nearby. Near one end of the room sat a huge desk with two lit-up computer screens. A high-backed, overstuffed office chair, its back to the boys, faced both screens.

Chris and Gordie stood frozen at the door, unable to take their eyes off the high-backed chair.

"This is like *Psycho*," Gordie whispered nervously. "The rocking chair scene."

"Except there's nobody in this chair," Chris said, straightening to his full height.

"We hope," Gordie said.

Chris stepped further into the room, shuffling sideways toward the library table as he kept an eye on the chair.

"See anybody?" Gordie whispered.

Chris shook his head. He motioned Gordie to come in and check the other end of the room. Gordie tiptoed in.

"Find anything?" someone said.

Both boys jumped, their hearts skipping.

"Well?" Teddy repeated from the door. "Did you find anything?"

Gordie and Chris turned and saw Teddy framed by the door, Vern peeking over his shoulder. But there was no movement from the chair. Chris blew out a sigh of relief.

"Geez, Teddy. You scared the crap out of us," he said.

"Sorry. We didn't find a thing upstairs. How about you?"

"Not yet. I think this room is our best bet. Help us look, fast. She may be back soon."

Teddy and Vern stepped in, as if waiting for directions.

"Hey, look at the computer," Vern said. "It's doing things."

Everyone looked. The computer screen on the right darkened and brightened ever so slightly as words, then sentences, then paragraphs appeared. But there was no clickity-clickity sound of fingers pecking at a keyboard.

"Is it a message from somewhere?" Vern said. "Like a telegram?"

"I don't think so," Chris said. ""It's been doing that since we got here." He worked his way around the library table and eased close enough to look past the high-backed chair at the screen. Then he looked down at the chair.

"Gordie. You guys," Chris gasped. "You gotta see this!"

There in the high-backed chair sat a slumped-over Stephen King, hands crossed on his lap, chin on his chest, Coke-bottle eyeglasses hanging askew from one ear.

"Oh my God. Is he dead?" Vern said. "He's dead, isn't he? I just knew it."

The words and sentences continued to appear on the screen.

Then, a snore. From Stephen King. And another snore. The writer's head lifted slightly as air expanded his chest and pushed up his chin. The man had shorts on.

"Look at that," Teddy said, pointing to what looked like a telephone line clipped into the meaty part of King's forearm. Wrist restraints bound his arms to the chair and a chest strap held him in the sitting position. An IV bottle hung from a hook between the two computer screens, its fluids dripping through a plastic hose and disappearing under a piece of gauze taped to King's thigh. Had they found King's journal, his repository of ideas, hanging from a hook?

"The cable goes to the computer," Chris said. "There's another one in the other arm, too." The second cable disappeared behind the computer, too. Words and sentences kept materializing on screen at a steady pace.

"You're closest, Gordie," Chris whispered. "What's it say?"

Gordie stared at the screen. "It looks like part of a story. Dialogue between characters. Now it's stopped. The writing's stopped." Gordie turned and looked back at his friends, then down at Stephen King in the chair. King's eyes were closed.

"Look," Chris said. "The writing's started again."

Gordie turned to the flickering screen. "It says *I know you little turds are in the room. I can hear you. I'd like to grab you and beat your little asses, but I'm not allowed to move my muscles just yet because of the IV drugs. Once Tabby unhooks me, though, you're going to be damn sorry you ever broke into my house!*"

"Who's Tabby?" Vern said.

"Tabby, you dimwit! Tabitha, his wife. Once she unhooks that thing and the wires," Chris said, "he'll come after us."

"Who'll come after us?" Vern said.

"Him!" Teddy shouted, pointing at the man in the chair. "Stephen King. But he can't move until she unhooks him."

King snored again. The computer screen flickered.

"What's it say, Gordie?" Teddy said.

"It says, *Chris Chambers, I killed you off in my story, The Body. In Rob Reiner's movie version, Stand By Me, he has Richard Dreyfuss, the narrator, reveal it at the end. In fact, I wrote how all your lives turned out.*"

A look of horror came over Chris's face, and Gordie blinked as if he'd just been punched in the stomach.

"What's he talking about?" Teddy said.

"Shut up, Teddy," Gordie said. His eyes had the same determined look as that day out on the Back Harlow Road when he'd faced down Ace Merrill as Ace held a switchblade to Chris's throat.

"Gordie?" Chris choked out. "What's he mean, he killed me off?"

"Chris, shut up!" Gordie said. "Everything'll be okay."

A string of fresh words flickered onto the screen. *Your days are numbered, boys. Wait till Tabby gets home.*

"You guys get out of here," Gordie said. And when they didn't move, "Now!"

Chris, Teddy, and Vern backed out of the room.

Gordie stepped to the desk, touched the asdf keys on the computer keyboard, and *asdf* appeared on the screen.

What in hell do you think you're doing, Lachance? appeared in response.

Gordie typed *So you're ultimately the one who killed my brother Denny. And you're the one who killed Ray Brower with the train.*

What are you talking about? It's fiction. They're stories, Lachance.

Well, Mr. King, maybe I'll just interrupt your writing with a little fiction of my own. I'm a writer, too, you know.

You're not a writer. You're a character, a fictional kid who's supposed to grow up and become a fictional writer. But you have no life beyond that one story.

Gordie typed *Stephen King was walking along the road near his lake house in western Maine when a van came over the hill, its driver a man who had been convicted many times of drunk driving. The man's dog stood up in the van's passenger seat and tried to climb onto the man's lap. The man took his eyes off the road as he tried to push the dog away. The movement of his right hand caused his left hand to pull the top of the steering wheel further right. The van swerved onto the shoulder of the road and struck Stephen King with more than enough force to kill him.*

Stephen King interrupted, words appearing on screen. *You can't do this.*

Watch me Gordie wrote. Gordie placed a hand on the computer mouse, pointed the cursor at File and clicked the drop-down menu.

Stop! Please! appeared on the screen. *How about this? Chris Chambers didn't die after all. His death by stabbing was mistakenly reported. He survived the wounds.*

Gordie's fingers flashed over the keyboard. *Stephen King also survived his.* Then he pointed the cursor arrow at Save and clicked. He withdrew the diskette and put it in his pocket.

Twenty minutes later, while Tabitha King disconnected her husband's IV and unclipped the cables from his forearms, four crew cut boys followed the tracks past the Bangor City Limits. The round-faced boy chomped on a candy bar and the kid with the deformed ear made machine gun noises. The other two simply talked, occasionally putting their arms over each other's shoulders the way best friends often do.

"Hey! Hey, guys!" the chubby boy suddenly called out. "The Holy Grail! We forgot to get Stephen King's journal!"

The other three looked at him, shook their heads, and in unison said, "Vern!"

A battery-operated radio hung from a tomato stake near where a woman knelt weeding in her garden. One song faded out and a new one faded in, an oldie. First came the throbbing strings of the bass. Plunk-plunk-plunk, plunk. Plunk-plunk-plunk, plunk. Then the sandy rasp of castanets or perhaps brushes on drums.

A tinkling bell. Guitar. And the at-first piercing, then smooth, sweet voice of Ben E. King. *When the night … has come …and the land is dark … and the moon … is the only … light we'll see … No, I won't … be afraid …Oh, I-ah-ah-ah won't … be afraid … just as long … as you stand … stand by me.*

THE SWIMMER

I HAVEN'T SWUM in Plock's Boat Basin since I was twelve. Haven't dared.

It was a hot day in mid July 1961. Our regular gang—11, 12, 13 years old—had gathered by the old oyster factory buildings on Fifth Street (where the condo complex is now). The boat basin and the oyster factory had boomed in the earlier part of the century, but by 1961 the oyster industry had practically died out. Plock's Basin remained home to the tired old survivors of the shrunken oyster fleet.

Most people who wanted to go swimming didn't go near Plock's. If they were interested in family beachgoing, they went to sandy, shallow Gull Pond on the bay or to Clark's Beach or Town Beach on Long Island Sound. Those were the best beaches for sunbathing and regular old *swimming*. But for us kids, what was important was not just swimming but *deepwater* swimming—and *diving*. We needed a place where we could play water tag and run and dive and swim in deeper water and be outrageous. That's what Plock's little boat basin offered us.

Walled in on three and three-quarter sides by high wooden bulkheads, with only a few oyster boats tied up, Plock's was heaven. The basin was six to twenty feet deep at mid-tide, a hundred yards across by a hundred fifty yards long. We could dive either from the boardwalk docks or from the decks and cabins of the oyster boats. Plock's Basin was the place to be.

On this particular day, temperatures had soared to almost a hundred, and no one thought about anything except getting into the water. There were nine or ten of us there at first, and we played odd-finger to see who would be "it" first in water tag. The only real rule we had was that there was no tag-back. If you were "it" and you tagged somebody, they couldn't tag you back right away, they had to find somebody else. It wasn't the ideal solution to the problem of picking on the weakest link, but it was helpful.

My cousin Chuck was "it" to start, and everybody had a head start, racing around the boardwalks, jumping onto the boats, diving into the water. But after a couple of minutes Chuck caught up to our friend Ramon and tagged him, which—because of the no tag-back rule—gave Chuck a rest and put Ramon on the offensive. Ramon went after my other cousin Spider, but Spider was too quick for him. So Ramon (this may have been part of his strategy) gave a quick feint like he was going for Spider again, then made a sharp turn and came barreling toward me.

Luckily I had a couple of steps on him and raced up a ladder onto the cabin of one of the oyster boats. When he was almost all the way up the ladder I made a long high dive, stretching out like Rocky the Flying Squirrel, covering as much distance as I could toward the middle of the basin. While airborne I had no idea whether Ramon had broken off the chase or would follow and try to catch me in a stretch swim.

I kept my hands together over my head to streamline my entry into the water, and just before I sliced through the water's surface *I saw a face below me.* It was the size of a human's but looked more like the ugly toadfishes we sometimes caught off the dock. It stared

THE SWIMMER

up at me, not from the top of the water like someone treading water, *but from beneath,* grinning hideously. My heart leapt and I gasped, sucking in my breath even deeper than I had planned. My momentum carried me five feet beyond the grinning face. As soon as I hit the water, knowing what was behind me—not Ramon but this scariest of all Halloween masks—I flapped my arms down toward my sides to propel me forward, pushing as much water as I could with my palms, hoping to gain speed and distance on the trip across the basin.

Oddest Yet ⚡ STEVE BURT

My aim was to surface fast and start stroking over-hand. Before I could, while I was still in my glide, I opened my eyes. There, face-to-face, body-to-body with me, as if he were my mirror image—no more than six inches separating us—was the being, the thing. I made out fuzzy arms—in salt water nothing is perfect-ly clear—and hands that appeared to be webbed. Its eyes glowed like hot coals—first glowing, then fading, then glowing, then fading again—pulsing at almost the same rate as my heart, which was super fast. It must have had flippered feet, because it wiggled the way a mermaid might, not needing to use its arms or webbed hands to keep up.

I don't know if it was staring at me or mocking me. I kept stroking my frogman stroke—hands overhead then down to the sides—while furiously kicking with my legs and feet. I had no idea if the thing meant me harm. All I knew was, I needed to get out of the water—I needed to get *above* the water, fast.

I tried to angle up toward the surface where I could catch my wind and stroke for the other side of the basin. *But I wasn't surfacing.* I was moving forward, but I wasn't surfacing. *Something was holding the belt buck-le of my cut-offs, anchoring me by the very center of my body.* And I could feel—*pressing against my stomach*—the knuckles of the thing's thick webbed fingers. I closed my eyes, hoping it was a bad dream, a night-mare, and prayed it might disappear. But when I opened them, the creature was still there, glaring. It occurred to me then that my arms and legs had ceased to move, yet the creature and I were traveling forward at the same rate of speed, propelled by its strong legs. It must have seen my terror then, because the thing tilted its head ever so slightly and looked at me—*was it puzzled?*—then released its grip and broke off to my right, toward the channel that led from the basin to the open bay.

I surfaced, gasping, gulping down air. My eyes searched frantically for sight of my friends. I yelled, "Everybody out of the water, quick!"

I glanced toward the channel opening, expecting to see, I suppose, something like a shark's dorsal fin, or a leaping porpoise, or the snorkel of a scuba diver, something. Instead I saw only a wake, like the wake of a torpedo in a war movie. I continued my swim across the basin, slowly now.

Ramon was fifty yards behind, catching up. He had hit the water only a few seconds behind me and should have only been ten yards back. But somehow I had gained forty yards—*underwater*—without stroking, in a flash.

"How'd you get so far so fast?" he called out. "Flippers?"

I didn't answer. I grabbed the knotted rope hanging from one of the boats and pulled myself aboard. Then I yelled again, "I'm serious, everybody, stay out of the water. Something down there—something like the Creature from the Black Lagoon—grabbed me by the belt and pulled me along. If it hadn't let go, I'd have drowned."

Everybody laughed at first. But the more I tried to convince them I was deadly serious, the more they listened. Unfortunately, the more they questioned me, the more the thing began to change in my mind to a dolphin or a shark. That was okay, though, so long as it kept them out of the water.

Three weeks later I read in *The Suffolk Times* that a couple of boys ventured too far from shore near Fifth Street Point, not three hundred yards from the channel to Plock's Basin. As their mothers watched from the beach in horror, the boys were swept away in a vicious riptide. The mothers screamed when they saw the boys go under. Two minutes later, miraculously, both boys were found, not drowned, but exhausted and safe, clinging to the end of the Fifth Street dock. A giant frogman, they swore, had towed them to safety—one boy in each webbed hand. No one else saw it happen, though. No creature. No wake. I phoned the boys and shared my story. But that's as far as it went. We didn't convince any adults.

There were no other incidents around Greenport that summer—none that were made public, anyway. In late August, *Newsday* reported an incident a hundred miles west at Jones Beach. A lifeguard trying to save a drowning girl found himself caught in an undertow. Before he blacked out, he saw something shadowy face-to-face, something with glowing eyes. It grabbed him by the front of his swimming trunks, he swore. Next thing he knew, he and the little girl were waking up on shore. More than a hundred people claimed they saw both the lifeguard and the little girl come shooting up onto the beach like torpedoes. But no one saw the source.

I'm mostly convinced the thing I met that July day was benevolent, not evil. But just the same, I haven't swum in Plock's Basin—or in any salt water for that matter—since that day. And now that I've told the story again for the first time in forty-three years—told it and felt the chills up my backbone, told it and remembered those horrible glowing eyes and that frightening face, I don't think I ever will again.

POWER OF THE PEN

THEY HAD ALWAYS BEEN CLOSE, this brother and sister. But then, too, they'd always been competitive, and for the most part in their growing-up years she had bested him. Now they were in their thirties and each living comfortably on the inheritance from their deceased parents.

She continued to live in their hometown of Salem, Massachusetts, writing her poetry and venturing out only occasionally for church or to attend a meeting of the Board of Directors for Salem's Witch Museum. He, on the other hand, had moved away to a small town near Lancaster, Pennsylvania, in Amish Country. He hadn't joined the Amish, but he did appreciate their simple lifestyle. So, although they had gone in different directions, this brother and sister still had some similarities, preferring the simple, reclusive lifestyle.

They had not seen each other in a number of years. Was it four? Or five? But they kept in touch by letter several times a week. Time and distance had helped them forget some of their differences, and in an odd way, not seeing each other regularly had perhaps deepened their relationship.

Thursday, September 2
Dearest sister,

    My job at the library goes well, even if only part time. I enjoy being amongst the books and find that I love the relative quiet of the place. The interaction I have with patrons is pleasant. There is of course the usual small talk as they bring in books or check them out. And because I'm only there 16 hours a week, this being a small-town library, I find the demands of the job not too taxing. The obvious bonus is, I become familiar with more books than I would if I were only a patron of the library. My only regret must be that my life will surely end before I can read all the books I'd like to read. For the first time in a long time, I feel happy, almost content (and perhaps that too will come).

    I appreciated the last poem you sent. It was an excellent piece of work and conveyed much deep feeling. If I were to critique any part of it, it would be the last line, the sense of which may be a bit unclear to the reader. That occurs, I think, because of the forced rhyme on the last word. I know you are sensitive about your poems, but I trust this comment will help your work to be even finer than it already is.

I hope your work with the board at the Witch Museum continues to be fulfilling.

Your loving brother,
Robert

∧∧∧∧∧∧

Wednesday, September 8
My dear little brother,

I am happy to hear that your new job at the library suits you. While it may be a basic clerk's position, there is no shame in that. If anyone were to ask me, I would assure them that our parents' fortune provides you with more than adequate income, and that the library position is more a public service on your part, much the same as my agreeing to sit on the Board of Directors at the Witch Museum.

I will take your critique of my poem's last line under consideration.

Yesterday several of us from the Board of Directors attended a lecture and demonstration given by a modern witch at the Museum. The woman looked to be a hundred years old and claimed she was closer to two hundred. She cast a few spells. There was quite a large group from the public in attendance and the spells were a hit.

My only regret is that I sat in the front row. The room was warm, so we had the overhead fans on. During one particular spell the fan above me blew some of the powder in my direction, causing me to sneeze seven times. I have never sneezed seven times in succession in my entire life, and when I sneezed the seventh time, the witch gave me the strangest look and said, "Seven. Seven only. Seven." I have no idea what she meant, and when I pressed her about it afterward, she refused to explain further.

The sneezing episode brought to mind how sick you were from the influenza that winter you were eight and I was nine. Oh, how I worried about you then. That same year, you'll recall, in the summer and fall, we played croquet with Mom and Dad almost every afternoon. After what must have been five hundred games, you finally beat me for once. You played well, though I recall that you won by a lucky shot, your ball striking a rock that diverted it into the final post. Then you crowed mercilessly about your victory the entire rest of the day.

I will send another of my poems, but not with this letter, perhaps with the next. I have a little tweaking to do on it first.

Your loving sister,
Elizabeth

∧∧∧∧∧∧

Monday, September 13
Dearest sister,

So strange, you sneezing exactly seven times. (I've been sneezing a lot lately, too, and may have a touch of the flu.) Obviously the witch's powder was an irritant to your mucous membranes. You don't think it was in any way toxic, do you? Has it continued? Have you manifested other symptoms? Perhaps you should consult Dr. Mather, just to be certain there are no long-term effects. I hate to be a worrywart about your health, but you know I've always been a bit of a hypochondriac myself. Please take care of yourself.

Me? I'm healthy as a horse, finally. I'm trying to learn to be more social, but it's not easy. At my boss's suggestion

I tried out for a bit part in a small skit we're doing as a fundraiser here at the library. Guess what? I got the part. It's only two lines, but all the same I'm excited about it. Imagine, your brother, the thespian!

I look forward to receiving another of your poems.

Your loving brother,

Robert

∿∿∿∿∿

Saturday, September 18

My dear little brother,

No need to worry, the sneezes stopped at seven. Thank you for your concern.

Good luck with the little play. I'm surprised you tried out for a part (and more surprised you got it). Until now the only acting I'd ever seen you do was acting innocent, like the time Mom accused me of stealing her pie from the windowsill. You let her punish me instead. Good luck with the acting. As they say in the theater, break a leg.

I've enclosed the new poem I promised you. I like it quite well myself.

Your loving sister,

Elizabeth

∿∿∿∿∿

Friday, September 24

Dearest sister,

Sorry to be so long answering your letter, but the day I received it I actually broke my leg. I tripped over a foot-stool during rehearsal and tumbled off the stage. It was a nasty compound fracture, the shinbone protruding through a bloody mass of flesh. But the doctors set it and it's in a cast. After a couple of days in the hospital, now I'm laid up in my apartment. Luckily, friends from the library look in on me daily and bring in meals. They've gotten another fellow to take my part in the play. Such a brief career on stage, eh? Oh well. The upside of it is, I'm learning what community is really about.

I loved the poem you sent, though I found it hard to focus at first (because of my leg pain mostly, not because of any problem with the poem). I wonder if it wouldn't be stronger if you switched the second and fourth lines of the fifth stanza? It would keep the rhyme scheme the same, but it would clarify the point about the barns. I read it aloud to one of the women who stopped by with a meal, and she agreed.

The leg is starting to ache again, so I'll sign off for now.

Your loving brother,
Robert

/\\/\\/\\/\\/\\/\\

Wednesday, September 29
My dear little brother,

Thank you for the suggestion you and your woman friend made regarding my poem. In the future, please don't show my work to anyone else.

A broken leg? You should have had someone notify me when it happened. When you're out and about and have a little time, please file some papers regarding next-of-kin and all that, just in case something happens. I have already done it on my end. And I have had Mr. Higgins, Mom and Dad's lawyer, draw up a will for me.

Do you remember Mrs. Merritt's husband Lester who lived two streets behind us? Three weeks ago he took a fall in the barnyard and broke his leg, too, a compound fracture, just like yours. He had been recuperating at home but gangrene set in (the wet, not the dry, so there was not only infection but fear of blood poisoning). They took him to the hospital to treat him. But so much of his lower leg was dead flesh they had to amputate it at the knee.

I'm glad you're becoming more sociable, though I'm sorry it took a broken leg for you to get to know your neighbors.

Your loving sister,
Elizabeth

Friday, October 8
Dearest sister,

I've developed gangrene and am writing this as I wait for an ambulance to come and transport me to the hospital. They're going to try massive doses of some drug on me, but the doctor has confided that there's a good chance they'll have to amputate my leg at the knee. I'm devastated at the thought but also thankful they can do the surgery here (if needed) on short notice. I'm keeping my fingers crossed that the drugs will work. But if I must choose between my leg and my life, let them take the leg.

This will be my last letter from the apartment for a while. I'll have someone pick up my mail and will send you the hospital address soon. Telephone me there after you get my letter. I don't know the number.

Your loving brother,
Robert

Wednesday, October 13
My dear little brother,

I telephoned you at the hospital last night, but the nurse on duty said you were sedated so you could sleep. (Better than being in a coma.) She said you'd had the surgery for amputation at the knee, and that it was a success.

But she said you'd be experiencing a lot of pain during recovery (which reminded me of you laughing cruelly when my throat was so sore after the tonsillectomy). This is all so hard to take. Gangrene. Losing part of a leg. It's very upsetting to me. I'll mention you during our prayer meeting at church tonight.

The nurse suggested I try phoning you today at noon, that you might be awake at lunchtime. I'll take her advice and will try. In the meantime, I'll keep doing what I know best, writing. At least I can keep up my end of the correspondence.

The postman is due any time, and I want to get this in the mail. I've enclosed a new poem. I'd appreciate your comments.

Your loving sister,
Elizabeth

∧∧∧∧∧∧∧∧

Wednesday, October 13
My dear little brother,

My second letter today. I'm worried. When I telephoned a few minutes ago, the nurse put your doctor on and he said you had slipped into a coma. He said a coma is the brain's way of protecting the body while it heals. I asked the doctor if I should come and be by your bedside; he said to give it another day first. He promised to phone me tomorrow.

In the meantime I'm a wreck. I feel like I did when we had that picnic on the Charles River, when Mom made me watch over you. You disappeared and I called out for you again and again until I was hoarse. I begged you to stop hiding, to stop being so mean to me, but you wouldn't come out. When you finally did, you were laughing, you were horrible. I know this is a coma and it's serious, but you'd better not be toying with me *again. Sometimes you make me so angry.*

I'm off to town for groceries, so I'll mail this at the Post Office.

> *Your loving sister,*
> *Elizabeth*

P.S. Poor Mr. Merritt died a couple of days ago. His funeral was yesterday.

Thursday, October 14
My dear brother,

I can't go anywhere for fear I'll miss a call from your doctor. I'm too worked up to read a book or work on a poem. There's not much to do while waiting except to write another letter. I tried knitting, but as I knit I find myself counting to seven over and over. It only serves to remind me of the seven sneezes. I've been trying to remember how many letters I've written you since the sneezes. If you were awake, you could tell me.

As I promised, I lifted up your name at prayer meeting last night. Afterward, Rev. Decker asked if I'd like a pastoral visit. He had been planning to see Mrs. Merritt this morning anyway and said he could swing by. He just now telephoned from the Merritts' to say he's on his way here now. I've got to put on the tea kettle, so I'll close this letter and put it out for the postman.

> *Your loving sister,*
> *Elizabeth*

Friday, October 15
My dear brother,

When the doctor called yesterday morning to say you had died, I couldn't believe it. My mind refused to grasp it.

Oddest Yet ⚡ STEVE BURT

I felt a wave of guilt. Did I somehow contribute to your accident, your infection, your coma? Your death? I never even said goodbye.

Since then I've dwelt upon the witch's words. Seven, she said, seven. And so, this letter (I believe) being my seventh since the spell was cast, and having no other hope, I offer you the words Rev. Decker shared from scripture this morning.

He rose from the dead.

Love,

Elizabeth

∿∿∿∿∿∿

She sealed the letter and carried it to the front porch for the postman to take. Then she went inside and waited for the phone to ring, for the doctor to call and babble on about a miraculous recovery.

Instead, she heard heavy footsteps on the porch. Her skin broke into goosebumps as a terrifying image flashed across her mind. Her heart fluttered errantly for a moment and she put a hand to her chest. The other hand she placed on the deadbolt and unlocked the door. She could picture the letter where she had hung it by a clothespin from the mailbox. Could she still snatch it and tear it up? Would it make a difference? She turned the knob and tried to prepare herself for what she might see, praying to God it was only the postman, an hour early.

UNCLE BANDO'S CHIMES

UNCLE BANDO WASN'T REALLY MY UNCLE. He was no blood relative at all. Nor was he an uncle in the friend-of-the-family sense, like Uncle Red, Dad's high school best friend who still came over on Monday nights to play poker. I never even knew if Bando was a first name, a last name, or a nickname. I just knew he was our neighbor the three years we lived on Foster Street when I was growing up.

A tiny, ancient man only slightly taller than I was at ten, he looked either Oriental or Middle Eastern, I'm not sure which—I suppose because of his darkish skin, gray pointed goatee, and pigtail down the middle of his back. But when I asked him about it one day as we planted corn in his backyard garden, he said no, he wasn't any of those. He didn't volunteer anything more about his background, and I didn't press him. I can't remember when it was that I started calling him Uncle Bando—I suppose it must have been when I first met him, when I was eight—but he seemed to like it and didn't discourage me.

Uncle Bando never seemed to have a job he had to go to. Maybe he was retired. I don't know. But he did make hanging things in his apartment: chimes, mobiles, reflecting prisms. He called them all *catchers*—light, sound, and wind catchers—and they hung everywhere, in every room, over his garden, in his windows. I especially liked the light-catchers, with shards of glass that bent and spread out the light into rainbows on the walls.

The sound-catchers were mostly made of metal. One set looked like miniature polished brass gongs on filament wire. Another was constructed from silver coin-sized disks suspended by dental floss. Once, after I'd brought him apple pies from my mother several weeks in a row, a pie-tin mobile appeared inside his front door. It wasn't exactly musical, and when the pie tins struck each other, they thudded and clanked.

My favorite, though, wasn't a sound-catcher. It was one of the simplest light-catchers Uncle Bando ever made—four cut-out lids from tin cans and suspended on strings that hung down from a small cross of balsa wood. I suspected the string and balsa wood had come from a kite I'd crashed into a tree and later thrown into the trash.

Whenever I visited Uncle Bando, every hanging thing seemed to shimmer or tinkle or sparkle or spin. The apartment felt as if it had a life of its own, as if there were spirits alive there. Even in the winter, when there were no windows or doors open, Uncle Bando would create his own air currents by burning candles under his catchers, keeping them both enlightened and enlivened.

For my tenth birthday my mother was planning to take me to the Bronx Zoo. But the night before my birthday, Mom got the flu. Uncle Bando, who seldom left his apartment, volunteered to fill in and take me. He said he had a catcher for someone.

We left at 9:30 that morning and stopped at Grossman's Deli for a bagel. As I stood waiting for Mr. Grossman to hand me my change, I was conscious that a huge fish had been laid out on ice in the display case behind me. The hairs on the back of my neck prickled, so I turned around. Just the fish, the dead fish, its eyes dull. Then I heard Mr. Grossman say, "Here's your change, son," and as I spun to face him, I caught a reflection in the mirror behind him. It was the fish, but its eyes didn't show dullness. Only terror. The eyes screamed something worse than death. My own eyes flew open so wide I couldn't blink. I shuddered, spun, and reeled out the door, leaving Mr. Grossman calling, "Your change, son! Your change!" Uncle Bando got it to me later, before we got to the subway entrance.

Near the subway turnstiles stood four men in black jackets, leaning against the wall, cigarettes dangling from their mouths. One of them watched me through narrow eyes as I put my token in the turnstile and walked through. The hair on my neck prickled again the way it had with the fish, so I looked away and hurried toward the train platform. Uncle Bando's legs were short and old, and he was slow. I had to wait. He carried a gift-wrapped box under his arm, a box the size a Macy's shirt might come in. I wondered whom the package might be for, and where we'd have to stop to deliver it.

The train ground to a stop in front of us and the doors flew open. We stepped on and Uncle Bando sat down first, in a seat practically at the center of the car. I sat on his left. Uncle Bando sat quietly, gift box across his knees, hands on top, his eyes closed as if in prayer or meditation.

Two seventyish women sat opposite us, one reading *People*, the other holding a navy blue sweater across her lap to cover her pocketbook. Sweater Lady stared at a point on the floor somewhere between herself and us. Her look of seeming boredom reminded me of my mother's cautions about eye contact, so I too looked down for a moment. I wondered if Sweater Lady hadn't been mugged. She appeared to be an experienced subway traveler.

At the front of the subway car sat a bushy-haired, redheaded woman in a Hunter College sweatshirt. Her jeans were torn at the knees and she had a pair of well-worn leather sandals strapped to her feet. She carried no pocketbook, knapsack, or book bag, and sat with her legs crossed and a pencil in her right hand, working intently on a crossword puzzle magazine as if it were a school assignment she had to finish. Another experienced subway traveler.

At the back of the subway car sat a black couple with heads of silver hair that practically shone like angels' halos. They held hands. Their gaze jumped from person to person. I supposed they were searching out danger. They were either inexperienced or once-burned riders. The man's free hand rested on the head of a cane in front of him. She clutched a white purse. I imagined for a moment that his cane hid a sword, and her handbag a derringer.

The sound of the doors starting to close drew my attention. I looked in time to see a pair of hands grasping the doors and throwing them back open. The four men in leather jackets stepped in, doors closing behind them. The one who had watched me pass through the turnstile looked straight at me and curled his lips into a frightening smile. My blood froze and I dropped my gaze to the floor again. The four pairs of black boots went to different parts of the subway car. The train lurched out of the station, picked up speed and settled into its slight side-to-side rocking rhythm. The interior lights flickered from time to time.

The man who had watched me at the turnstiles stood gripping the rider-support pole three feet in front of me. Without looking above his waist, I stole a glance around. The tallest of the four, pimple-faced with greasy black hair, took a seat opposite the young woman working the crossword. He stared, something she must have sensed, but she didn't look up, keeping her face in the puzzle.

The second man, with long eyelashes and a long nose, stood over the woman in the sweater and the one reading *People*. He sat beside the sweater lady, making sure his legs flopped apart so that his right one rubbed up against hers. She pulled away but failed to make any eye contact. He held his ground but didn't push things.

The third man, barrel-chested like a wrestler, had a tattoo on the back of his left hand, a mermaid. He sat next to but not touching the silver-haired black woman. She tensed and scrunched closer to her husband, whose fingers tightened on the cane. The two of them stared straight ahead, mouths tightly shut.

Disregarding my mother's warnings, I tried to sneak a look up at the man in front of me. He caught me looking and his gaze turned me to stone. His skin was pale, his cheeks hollow. I could feel the cold coming from his eyes. I couldn't look away. Uncle Bando's warm touch on my hand freed me.

"It's okay," Uncle Bando said, patting the back of my hand with his palm.

The lights flickered and the subway train clanked along, holding us in its swaying grip. I prayed we'd reach our stop quickly.

"Whatcha got, rabbi?" a ratchety voice above us barked. It was Cold Eyes.

The crossword girl sneaked a glance in our direction. Pimple Face caught her looking, smiled sadistically, and drawled, "Good book, huh, honey?" She quickly refocused on the magazine.

Uncle Bando closed his eyes again.

"I said Whatcha got in the box, rabbi?" Cold Eyes' voice was louder this time, less patient.

Uncle Bando opened his eyes, looked up. "Not a rabbi," he said calmly, then looked back down.

Cold Eyes stood still, at a loss for words, but only for a moment.

"Okay, then, Jew-bastard-not-a-rabbi!" he spat out, stretching to his full height, pulling his head back the way a cobra might before striking. "What's in the goddam box?"

The black couple and the guy with the tattoo snuck a look our way, their three heads turning in tandem the way front wheels on a car do.

Uncle Bando looked up at Cold Eyes, said calmly, "I'm not even Jewish," and looked back down.

Cold Eyes exploded, screaming, "What's in the goddam box, asswipe?" His eyes grew wide with rage and he ripped the box from Uncle Bando's grip. Everyone in the car turned to view the confrontation now. Cold Eyes tore at the wrapping paper, cursing the whole time. In no time the paper lay in a heap at his feet. He yanked back the top of the box to see what lay inside. Tissue paper over shiny metal. He peeled it back.

"What is it?" he demanded, gawking first at the item in the box, then at Uncle Bando.

"Wind chimes," I blurted, surprised at my own audacity. Seeing he still looked confused, I added, "Like a mobile, a musical mobile."

Cold Eyes stared at me. "Wind chimes?" he said dully. From the sound of his voice, it seemed he expected something more valuable in a gift box, or at least more practical. "Wind chimes?" he repeated in disbelief. Then, in a roar aimed at Uncle Bando, "Faggot chimes, you mean! Faggot chimes, Jew-boy!"

Pimple Face and Tattoo Guy laughed, and Long Nose joined in. Cold Eyes looked at each of them and laughed too, proud of himself for saying something either funny or terrifying or both.

"Faggot chimes! Faggot chimes!" Long Nose jeered.

Cold Eyes shot him a look, silencing him. Pimple Face and Tattoo Guy shut up, too, wiping away their smiles. The other passengers stared in terror at Cold Eyes. He was in charge. He turned back to Uncle Bando.

"So what're they for, Jew-boy?" Cold Eyes demanded, his lips curling into a sneer.

"Let me show you," Uncle Bando answered quietly. As he spoke, he pressed his palms down on his kneecaps and, with a rocking motion, started to rise from his seat.

"Sit down, asswipe!" Cold Eyes thundered shoving his hand against Uncle Bando's forehead and forcing him back onto the seat.

"No need for that, son," Uncle Bando said calmly. "I was simply going to demonstrate how you may use them."

"I know goddam well how to use 'em!" Cold Eyes snarled.

Uncle Bando offered Cold Eyes a weak smile. "Excuse me then, but perhaps when you asked, '*What* are they for?' you meant '*Whom* are they for?'" Uncle Bando asked the question so plainly that I couldn't tell whether he was being condescending or matter-of-fact. Cold Eyes heard him as condescending.

"You smart-ass little Jew bastard!" Cold Eyes raged, teeth clenched. Spittle dribbled off his lower lip, and I could see foam forming at the corners of his mouth.

"I'm not Jewish," Uncle Bando repeated.

I jumped to my feet. "He's not Jewish!" I said loudly.

A backhand slashed across my face and snapped my head to the side. Light flashed around me and momentarily I had no idea where I was. I tasted salty blood and my face ached.

Uncle Bando didn't move. I cowered beside him, but for an instant I wasn't sure I wanted to. He wasn't lifting a hand to defend me. But I had no one else.

"You little turd!" Cold Eyes screamed. "Keep your goddam mouth shut! If I say he's a Jew-boy rabbi, he's a Jew-boy rabbi. If I say he's a Flying Saucer, he's a goddam flying saucer. Got it?"

I nodded, terrified.

"So, old man," Cold Eyes said. "For *who* is the present?" He stood, waiting.

After a moment Uncle Bando said, "I made it especially for you."

Cold Eyes stared at Uncle Bando, unsure what the old man meant. He seemed to take it as a sign that Uncle Bando was finally kowtowing, that he finally was acknowledging that—at least on a subway far beneath the city—possession was indeed nine-tenths of the law and the wind chimes in Cold Eyes' hands now belonged to him.

"I thought you had, pops," Cold Eyes sneered. He reached into the box and lifted the catcher out. Only then I realized it wasn't a set of wind chimes. It wasn't a sound-catcher at all. It was a light-catcher, the one Uncle Bando had made from can lids and the string and balsa wood from my broken kite. The can lids shone like polished chrome hubcaps, each of the four lids hanging at a different height.

"There's no sound," Cold Eyes complained, his voice a spoiled child's. "The chimes don't hit together. They're strung out wrong. This is a piece of crap!"

"That's because this one's not actually a wind chime," Uncle Bando said softly. "It's for the light. It's a catcher, a different kind of catcher. And sometimes it's better to keep the four apart."

Cold Eyes raised his hand to strike Uncle Bando, and as he did, the car swayed and the interior lights flickered. For an instant, for the blink of an eye, it was pitch black. Then the lights were on again.

Cold Eyes was gone. So were his cronies. Vanished.

The rest of us sat wide-mouthed in disbelief. Then, hardly daring to move, we scanned the subway car. We just sat, our bodies caught in the car's sway. After a moment, the crossword girl and the woman with *People* magazine forced themselves to return to their magazines. The sweater lady looked back down at the floor. The black couple looked around the car cautiously. It was almost as if the four men hadn't been there. *Except I could still taste the salty blood in my mouth, could still feel my sore cheek.*

I looked to Uncle Bando. He held the catcher at arm's length, directly over the gift box. The four shiny disks turned lazily on the strings. Uncle Bando smiled at me, nodded, and shook his head sadly. One of the disks of the catcher glinted as it caught a shaft of light. For a split second I glimpsed what I'd seen in Mr. Grossman's deli mirror—the fish eyes—but it wasn't them, not the fish's. It was Cold Eyes, mutely screaming, begging, tortured mouth agape. He was caught in the can lid, trapped in Uncle Bando's catcher.

"Here's our stop," Uncle Bando said, depositing the catcher in the box and neatly folding the tissue paper over it, then securing the box lid.

"What about the catcher?" I asked, trying to blink away my shock.

"I'll keep it for the garden," Uncle Bando said, calmly smiling. "For the corn we planted. It'll scare the dickens out of those crows, don't you think?"

THE PRAYING MAN

EVERY MORNING JIMMY WALLACE and I walked to school together. To get there by foot we had to walk a long ways around one particular area, a bad neighborhood near the railroad tracks. It was either that or take the shortcut through it, which we often did. Taking the shortcut was a lot faster and felt more adventuresome.

One Monday in the fall we took the shortcut and, after we'd crossed the tracks and come to the first house—my parents called them tarpaper shacks, those tiny three-or-four-room frame houses—we noticed this old man in the window, sitting at his kitchen table with his hands clasped in front of him. His head was down, resting forward on his knuckles as if praying. Jimmy and I had seen other people do similar, and in fact both of us had at times done it with our own families, usually before dinner on Thanksgiving or Christmas or Easter. Except for those occasions and when we needed help getting out of tight spots, Jimmy and I weren't big on prayer.

Jimmy commented on the old man praying. And I think he made a joke about it: *You suppose he's praying for a bigger house?* Then we spotted a couple of kids coming in from a side street a block ahead, so we stretched our legs to catch up, forgetting all about the praying man in the window.

The next day we passed the tarpaper shack about the same time. The man was there again, head bowed, hands clasped, elbows on the table, forehead on his knuckles. We were pretty sure his eyes were closed—we tried not to be too obvious when we looked on our way past—and I supposed he might not be praying, but was instead bent over his morning newspaper, reading the way my father often did, while having a cup of coffee. As I recall, we made some comment about the praying mantis in the window, then headed for school.

On the third day the old man was there in his customary position, and I said to Jimmy maybe we should run a mirror in front of his mouth to see if there was any breath. Jimmy appeared puzzled, so I explained to him, you know, it's a way of checking to make sure a person's alive. It's what they do sometimes when they find a person lying corpselike in bed. Jimmy had never heard that before, and after forcing a belated chuckle, said "Maybe if he's there praying again tomorrow, we can try that."

The next day was Thursday, and the old guy was there again—or *still* there—praying or reading his newspaper or whatever. Curiosity got the better of Jimmy. He walked close to the window.

"Get out of there!" I said.

Jimmy raised his hand and rapped on the glass a couple of times.

The old man didn't move.

"Maybe he's deaf," I said, and Jimmy rapped again and flapped his arms this time.

Still no movement.

"Yeah," Jimmy said sarcastically. "He's deaf, all right. Or a very sound sleeper." He rapped a third time. "Maybe," he said, turning to me and saying what I hadn't dared to say, "Maybe the man's dead."

"Well, if he is," I said, "It's his business. Look and see if there's a newspaper on the table. Maybe he really is deaf and he's reading his paper at the same time every morning. Maybe he's engrossed."

Jimmy stared in through the window. "Matter of fact," he said, "There is a newspaper. And a green coffee mug. And a piece of toast. And a jar of jelly. And a butter dish. But I can't see inside the butter dish. It's got one of those covers that looks like a little coffin."

"Not funny!" I said. "Now come on! Let's go! Screw him. You can check him on the way home."

This would be the first day we'd pass the shack on the trip home, too. On Monday, Tuesday, and Wednesday we'd left school at dismissal and gone off to play sandlot football, the field being on the long route home. But this day, with all the Catholic kids getting out of school early for Catechism, there wouldn't be enough for a sandlot game. With no football, we'd take the shortcut home.

"Fine," Jimmy said. "We'll check on the way home." He stepped back and we headed for school.

By mid-afternoon the sun was reflecting off the shack window so we couldn't see in until we'd almost passed the house. Our deaf man—or dead man, our praying mantis—was still there.

"I think we better call the police," I said. "We need to report this."

"Not yet," Jimmy said. "Let me check one more time. I've never seen a dead person close up. This morning didn't count, because I wasn't sure he was dead. If he is, I want to see. You come with me."

My blood froze at the sound of his words. I just wanted to call the police and get it over with. If Jimmy simply wanted to buy a little time, fine, I wouldn't object. But I didn't want to go with him. The thought gave me the creeps. But I couldn't look weak in front of him, so I said, "Okay, but just for a minute. Then we go home and call the cops."

A moment later we were at the window gawking. On the table sat the green coffee mug, the toast, the jelly jar, the coffin-shaped butter dish, a vase of wilted flowers.

"Everything's where I saw it this morning," Jimmy said. "I'll bet it's been exactly like this all week, maybe longer. You know what's happened, don't you? The old man died reading the paper and drinking his coffee. He balanced in that position for a while and *rigor mortis* set in. I don't know how long it takes for that, but it set in, and now he's stiff as a board. They'll probably have to carry him out in that position, like furniture movers loading a statue."

The man's lap moved.

"Jesus!" Jimmy cried out, jumping back. "Did you see that?"

"Bet your ass I did," I said. "Let's get out of here."

"No, wait," he said. "Look. Look closer."

There, from under the edge of a small blanket on the man's lap, twitched something rope-like, black and white. A tail.

"It's a cat," I said. "The guy's dead, and his poor cat won't leave him. Let's go call the cops."

"Wait," Jimmy said. "What if there's something else in there—other cats or a dog or something, and they need help?"

"What if there are?" I said. "That's where the police come in."

"No," he said. "Let's check the door, see if it's open. We can call from inside."

Then it occurred to me what this was about. "It's not the cat you want to save, is it, Jimmy?" I said. "Or any other animals. You just want to see the dead guy up close. That's it, isn't it?"

"No. Not really," he said. "This is pretty close right here. That's not the reason."

"Oh, yeah? Then what is the reason?"

Jimmy didn't speak, but his silence told me.

"You want to touch him, don't you?" I said. "You want to touch the dead body."

His face reddened, and after a moment he said, "As a matter of fact, yes, I do. And there's nothing wrong with that. Kids our age are inquisitive, curious. And what's the harm?"

I didn't know how to answer that. It was a good question. What would be the harm?

"Besides," he said. "What if there are photographers? We want to be here if they take pictures, right? Can't you see the headlines? *Two seventh-graders discover dead body, rescue animals.* They'd have newspaper clippings of us posted all around school."

He had me off balance now, and the only thing I could think to say was, "We have to knock first."

"Of course," he said, and we moved onto a little porch. He knocked a half dozen times. No answer, so he turned the knob and opened the door. "Hello," he called. "Anybody home?"

We swung the door open and stepped in. It was a pigsty. Hundreds of newspapers, three-foot-high stacks of magazines, a coffee table piled high with dirty TV dinner trays, crusty silverware, and dusky glasses, clothing strewn over the couch, chairs, and end tables. The only sound was the hum of the refrigerator.

"This place smells worse than the dump," I said.

"I know," Jimmy said. "Dad said my grandfather's apartment was like this when they found him dead in bed last year. He turned into a packrat, lived on frozen dinners, soup, and Spaghetti-O's. I hadn't seen him in awhile. He lived next door to us for years when I was little, and before he moved away I used to visit him every day."

"Was that your first funeral?" I said.

"I didn't go. My parents thought it might be traumatic, so they left me with my aunt."

We waded through a sea of trash-filled paper bags to reach the door to the small kitchen where the praying man sat with his cat. Jimmy reached the doorframe before me and stood there. I knew he was staring at the old man's back the way I was staring at his. I was just as happy to have him block my vision. I was in no rush to get to the kitchen. I didn't want to look.

"What do you think killed him?" I said.

"Old age," Jimmy said. "Same as my grandfather. Body just wore out, or his heart, lungs, something. Like an old car that won't go any more."

The two of us stood in silence for a minute.

"Well, what're you going to do?" I said. "You going to touch him or not?"

Jimmy didn't answer for a long time. Then, softly, very softly, he said, "No. I don't think so."

"But are you sure he's dead?" I pressed.

"There's flies all over the toast," Jimmy said.

"What about the cat?" I said. "Wasn't that one of the reasons we came in?"

"I thought it was," Jimmy said. "But it wasn't."

There was something thick about Jimmy's voice, choked. I could only see the back of his head, couldn't see his face, but then it struck me—my friend was crying.

"You okay?" I said, half-afraid he might turn around and face me.

He tried to clear his throat, wanting to compose himself. But he didn't, didn't compose himself.

And when he didn't, I placed a hand on his shoulder and said with a knot in my own throat, "It's all right. It's okay." I felt his shoulder shake and I wanted to pull away, but I left my hand there.

THE PRAYING MAN

On the wall to Jimmy's left I saw a black telephone with a long tangled cord. For just a moment I thought about calling the police, who would arrive in no time. But I didn't.

"Let's go," I said. "We can call the cops from my house. We don't have to tell them we came in."

We waded through the garbage, closed the door, and went home to make the phone call. There was no photographer, no story, no mention of the squalid living conditions. All that appeared in print was an obituary: three paragraphs about an old man who loved his children, his grandchildren, his church, and his cat. Although we didn't speak about it then, I know Jimmy and I agreed it was all that needed to be said.

We haven't spoken of the incident since.

BAD DAY

THE ENGLISH MUFFINS stuck in the toaster and burned, the first sign that Bob Mintwax's day was going sour.

Bob dressed for work, couldn't find the tie he wanted though he searched high and low for it. Maybe he'd left it at the party he'd attended several days before—or was it the week before? He wasn't sure now. The missing tie seemed to be the second sign things were going bad, so he changed his shirt. He could use one of those other ties he owned, one that *sort of* matched.

When he finished dressing—although he wasn't totally comfortable with the look of his outfit—he slid into his overcoat, got into the Porsche, and headed for work. No, *not for work*—out of habit he'd started off in the direction of his old job—but downtown for an employment interview. This would be his sixth interview in two weeks. None had resulted in any kind of a callback for him. This wasn't easy, interviewing for jobs, not after having been in the computer software industry for fifteen years, the last eight as vice-president of the video games division. God, there'd been a lot of money in it for awhile, especially in developing interactive war video games for kids. The more violent, the more the kids liked them.

But here he was, off to another interview. This one sounded more promising, an Italian firm, Abruzzi's, which, at least on the surface, his research showed, appeared to be simply a string of bakeries around the Los Angeles area. A couple of Abruzzi's Bakeries had opened farther north and several had recently come on the scene down south in the San Diego area. But for the most part they were concentrated in L.A. and San Francisco.

Word on the street was that there was a Mafia connection. But Bob didn't see it, nothing obvious anyway. His friends had told him. But he found nothing in the newspaper archives or on the Internet about it. Because he didn't think he had much chance for the job anyway, nor much interest in working for a pastry company, he didn't bother investigating much deeper below the surface. Going on the interview would satisfy the bloodhounds at Unemployment.

When Bob arrived a pleasant receptionist—a blonde, not too awfully good-looking and a little on the chunky side—greeted him and motioned him to a seat.

"One of Mr. Abruzzi's associates will be with you in a moment," she said. "Make yourself comfortable. There are magazines on the table and the men's room is right down the hall." She pointed as she said it and went back to her filing.

Bob sat down and glanced at the stack of magazines. A recent *People* with Brad Pitt on the cover lay on top of the stack. He didn't bother examining the rest. He crossed one leg over the other knee, folded his hands in his lap and tried to appear calm and collected. There was no elevator music, no piped-in Muzak. The place was quiet except for the slight hum of the fluorescent lights. He watched his own crossed leg twitch slightly—up and down, up and down, up and down. This wasn't his nerves, he assured himself, it was simply the blood in his body pulsing normally through the arteries, and there was nothing he could do to stop the leg's movement even if he tried.

He closed his eyes and wondered what his wife Donna was doing—his ex-wife, that is, the one who'd just left him after twenty-two years. Things between them had deteriorated beyond the point of no return just about the time things started going downhill for him at the computer firm. But as his counselor pointed out, it was more likely things began deteriorating long before that, and Bob had failed to perceive the warning signs. By the time Bob did see them, it was too late, a full-blown crash. She moved out one day while he was at work; the divorce papers arrived the same day. Four months after that he'd gotten his pink slip at the firm.

To make matters worse—apparently trouble didn't come in threes, but in fives and sixes and sevens—his dog Butchy had been hit by a car, this barely three days after the pink slip. It happened early in the morning when he let the dog out to pee. Donna constantly warned him about letting the dog out the back without putting the prong collar around its neck. But when she was still living at home, he'd done it many times without incident. It was only for the two or three minutes while he put the morning coffee on. In the past Butchy had always been right there at the door, eager to come back inside for a drink of water from his bowl.

Damn it. Donna had been right. He hated to admit it, but she had been right. The poor dog had been loose and the poor dog had been hit. It was his fault.

That same night, the cat failed to return home. It was an indoor-outdoor cat, came in at night, spent most of its time at home inside during the day, and had learned to use a litter box. They'd had it for twelve or thirteen years, not terribly old for a cat, but not bad. Puffy, Donna called it, but he just called it Cat and pretended he didn't care for it. But now that it was gone he found that he did.

Did it die from a broken heart— for Donna, for Butchy? Or did it strike out on its own to seek its fortune? Maybe it just didn't want to spend any more time there with old goodtime Bob, living alone with him. Did it sense goodtime Bob's attitude, his depression, his blues, his gloom? Oh, woe is me, I have to live with Bob. Whatever. The damned cat had left.

And, as if the situation wasn't ludicrous enough, two days later Bob found the three goldfish floating in the top of the tank. He was sure he'd fed them, but maybe he hadn't. He'd been confused and depressed about so many things. Even so, it wasn't his fault. He couldn't help it if he'd been in a funk since Donna left and the dog died and the cat disappeared. He felt bad about the dog and the cat, but not the fish.

Maybe the fish simply committed suicide, held their breath, if fish can do such a thing.

"Mr. Abruzzi's associate will see you now," the receptionist's voice said, waking him out of what certainly could not be called a reverie.

He opened his eyes, saw the blonde—*would you call her full-figured; isn't that what you called heavier women?*—standing with her hands clasped in front of her, waiting patiently.

"Mr. Mintwax, are you all right?" she said.

He looked up, shook the cobwebs from his brain. "Yes, fine. Just thinking."

"If you'll follow me, Mr. Abruzzi's associate will see you now. His name is Mr. Tertullian."

Mr. Tertullian. Mr. Tertullian. Bob fixed the name in his head, tried to place it. *Wasn't Tertullian the name of a famous Roman orator or politician or writer or lawyer?* He couldn't remember where he'd heard the name before. *Tertullian. An emperor?* He'd probably seen it in one of those books with famous quotes alongside the text, like *The Keys to Abundant Living* or some such title.

One or two lines saved through history had no doubt been ascribed to this Tertullian fellow, who lived on and on through the quotes. The man never fully died; he lived on through literature first, now through self-help books. Ah, to be remembered forever. Tertullian.

He rose to follow the receptionist, wondering what Tertullian would look like. *An aquiline nose? A little crook to it? Ha-ha, a little crook, good Mafia joke. Medium height, well built, Italian? A Roman nose, not aquiline but Roman.* Something told him there was a difference. *Would he look like Tony Bennett in his fifties, or would the man be in his sixties? Dressed in a chef's white hat and smock? A pastry chef? Or would he be in a business suit? Would there be a bulge under his left arm from a shoulder holster? Would he be friendly? Would he be open?*

Bob Mintwax followed the receptionist down the hall, noticing its white walls and overhead acoustic tiles with fluorescents flush in the overhead. *Barely wide enough for two people.* Low ceiling. A smaller hallway than you'd find in a public school or a hospital. This felt constricting, as if it might double as a car crusher.

A moment later Bob found himself standing in front of a desk, looking across at a short, very fat, olive-skinned, black-haired man—*ah, there, the Roman nose*—a man in his fifties rising from behind the desk to shake his hand. He was at most five-feet-two, easily three hundred pounds. Bob heard the door click shut behind him and the receptionist was gone.

"Mr. Mintwax," the man said, motioning Bob to a seat. "Your resume is very strong. You've got a lot of experience in the computer industry, especially in computer video games."

Bob nodded.

"Can you tell me why you responded to our ad?" Tertullian said.

"Well," Bob answered. "It seemed to me that your ad was tailor-written for me. You asked for someone with experience in computers, particularly in computer video games. The ad came out only a couple of weeks after I had lost my own job due to my company's downsizing. I was vice-president of the entire division they eliminated, you know? I must say, though, when I read your ad I couldn't imagine why a bakery chain would be looking for a computer video games expert."

"Is there any particular reason they did away with your division?" Tertullian said, ignoring Mintwax's implied question.

Bob crossed his leg over his knee as he had in the waiting room. The top leg twitched, blood pulsing through the arteries.

"I wasn't privy to that," Bob said. "They didn't really let me in on that decision. They just said that they were doing away with the computer video games division."

Tertullian fixed Bob a hard stare. "Isn't it true, Mr. Mintwax, that the reason your division was downsized was because of a lawsuit brought against the company, wrongful death lawsuit concerning the deaths of three different teenagers in three different states—all by hanging? All suicides? All in basements?"

Tertullian didn't sound like a baker now, he sounded like a prosecutor on cross-examination.

"Well, uh," Bob stammered, lowering his eyes to his lap, noticing a stain on the tip of his tie. He also saw that he'd worn a brown belt with black pants. He'd meant to wear the black braided belt but couldn't find it. Like his favorite tie, the belt had disappeared. Bad things sure seemed to be coming in sevens and eights lately.

This interview isn't going well.

"I was aware that a lawsuit had been filed," he said, choosing his words carefully. "But I had no indication there was any connection between the lawsuit and the elimination of my division."

He looked back at Tertullian and tried to remind himself that this was an interview. *Sometimes*, he told himself, *job seekers have to answer a few uncomfortable questions that are on the prospective employer's mind. The secret is not to panic.*

Tertullian let the silence hang.

He's playing the waiting game, playing Chicken.

Bob noticed that behind the fat man there was a large mirror the size of a picture window. He could see himself and when he leaned slightly to the side he could see the back of Tertullian's head. Was it a two-way mirror, the kind they had in police interrogation rooms? He wondered if the big boss, Mr. Abruzzi, was behind it with some of his Mafia cronies. A ludicrous image popped into his mind—Abruzzi and three of his lieutenants, all in pastry chef outfits, with chef's hats on their heads and pastry guns in their hands, in a chorus line. He stifled a giggle.

"Something funny?" Tertullian asked sharply.

Bob looked appropriately apologetic. The interview had become uncomfortable enough that this seemed to him like a good time to turn things around. He'd go on the offensive. He could ask questions as well as Tertullian could. *Or maybe it's time to end the interview and get out.*

"Well, Mr. Tertullian, it just struck me as funny that a bakery—excuse me, a chain of bakeries—would be looking for someone with experience designing video games. As I said before, why would a bakery need that?"

Tertullian fixed him a serious stare

"We don't," Tertullian said coldly. "We don't give a rat's ass about designing video games."

Bob felt a chill. "Then why am I here?"

Tertullian leaned to his right, opened the bottom drawer of the desk, and withdrew something. It was a coil of rope with a noose in the end. The fat man carefully laid it on the green desk blotter between himself and Bob Mintwax.

Bob stared at it. It felt like a giant hand had gripped his heart and lungs and was squeezing.

"What's that for?" Bob said.

"An eye for an eye," Tertullian answered.

Bob stared, waiting for an elaboration.

Tertullian pushed the noose closer to Bob. "One of the three boys who hanged himself," the fat man said, "was Mr. Abruzzi's nephew, his baby sister's boy. Mr. Abruzzi believes there were some subliminal messages associated with the video game. It was a game you personally designed."

Bob moved his mouth, but no words came out.

Tertullian nodded toward the noose.

"Take it. Your life's a shambles anyway, Mintwax. Your wife left you, your dog died, your cat disappeared, your fish all went belly up. No job. What's left? You can't find a decent tie to match your suit, can you, or even a belt to match your trousers? I wouldn't be surprised if you found your Porsche's been sideswiped here in the parking area."

The color drained from Bob Mintwax's face. He sat slack-jawed.

"Take it," the fat man repeated, nodding at the noose. "It's a gift, our gift to you."

Bob tried to stand, but his legs were wobbly.

"Thinking about your parents in that retirement home in Florida, are you?" Tertullian said. "Well, don't worry. They're fine, perfectly fine. *For now*."

Bob's shoulders hunched forward. Tears of terror welled up in his eyes. The door opened behind him and two men walked in and stood on either side of him.

My associates will be happy to escort you to your car, Mr. Mintwax," Tertullian said. "Are you sure you're all right to drive? You don't look so steady, and we wouldn't want you to have an accident now, would we?"

The two men hooked Bob Mintwax under the armpits and helped him up. When they started for the door, Tertullian said, "Just a minute gentlemen. Mr. Mintwax forgot something."

Bob turned and saw Tertullian holding out the noose like a handshake. Any words Bob might have said caught in his throat.

"As I said," the fat man said. "Your parents will be fine, though they'll be sad to hear about the turn your life has taken lately."

Bob Mintwax shook off the two associates and wobbled out of the office into the narrow corridor. In one hand he held his resume, in the other the noose. He looked past the receptionist to the door. He could see his whole life lay behind him now.

What was that song title—*Nowhere to run, nowhere to hide?*

SHADOW MEADOW

JIMINY CRICKET AND I were on the way home from school one Friday afternoon when we decided to take a shortcut. The route would mean sprinting the Interstate and crossing a meadow we'd heard was haunted. We'd never gone that way before.

Jiminy Cricket wasn't my friend's real name, his real name was Jimmy. Critchlow. Jimmy Critchlow. But he was small and his name sounded like Jiminy Cricket from the Walt Disney thing, so everybody called him that.

I don't exactly know why we'd never taken the shortcut before, but that Friday we were determined to. It was a day when there'd been a little bit of snow on the ground, and there were reports from school bus drivers of black ice on the roads. But we figured the shortcut would save us 20 minutes getting home, closer to half an hour maybe.

The new route would take us behind the school and out through a stand of pine trees to the Interstate. We'd have to run pretty quick to make it across that, because it was always busy. Once across, though, we'd pass through a break of trees and take a leisurely stroll across the meadow.

We had no idea why people said the meadow was haunted—something about the spirit of a Revolutionary War soldier, we'd heard, a drummer boy not even full age, twelve or thirteen. Some said he

marched back and forth, others said he chased tres-
passers. But he never actually harmed anybody, at least
not so far as we could determine, so we weren't really
scared.

Jiminy and I headed through the pines, which pre-
sented no problem. It was a little slick underfoot, but
for the most part we simply left tracks in the snow. We
talked as we went, speaking of girls in our class and
sports, what we might do on the weekend if there was
enough snow still on the ground to go sledding. We
spoke a little bit about the history test we'd just had.
None of the conversation was all that heavy or conse-
quential.

In no time we reached the Interstate. There were
trucks flying by, a lot of tractor-trailers on the road, and
it looked like the pavement was fairly dry. So we braced
ourselves for a break in the action and, when the coast
looked clear, the two of us lit out for the other side,
crossing two lanes, then the median that had some
snow-covered grass in it. No problems. Rather than
slow down, since we were at a full tilt by then, we did
a quick on-the-run scan of oncoming traffic—a couple
of big trucks in the distance—and Jiminy called out, "If
we hurry we can make it."

So we just kept going. But the semis were barreling
along faster than we'd calculated, and we two hit a
patch of black ice. Our feet shot forward from under us
and we slid on our butts and backs, clunking our heads
on the pavement. Thank God our forward movement
carried us across the two lanes and onto the other
shoulder of the highway. I felt the breeze of the tractor-
trailers as they blew past.

"Whew! That was close," I said.

Jiminy said, "Too close for me. But I guess we made
it, didn't we?"

I looked at him and then myself and said,

"Apparently," and the two of us laughed.

"You hurt your head on the fall?" Jiminy said.

I felt the back of my head but didn't have any pain there. "Nope. I guess I'm okay. I know I cracked it pretty hard, but I must be okay. How about you?"

Jiminy felt his head and shook himself out to see if he had any bumps or bruises on the rest of his body, aches and pains, but there was nothing. "Nope, I'm fine," he said. "I just think we were pretty lucky. I don't think we'd better cut it that close again."

A minute or two later—maybe it was five minutes or ten, I don't know, time seemed a little funny—we found ourselves in the meadow. It was maybe a couple of football fields across and about the same distance long, nearly a perfect square but not quite. We could see several worn paths, the one we were on going down and forking out into a Y. According to our calculations we needed to take the path to the right, which would bring us across and out through a small stand of trees and onto Bommer Street. From there it was only six or seven blocks to home. It struck me funny that we'd never crossed this meadow as a shortcut to or from school before, and here we were in the eighth grade now.

As we walked across the meadow I spotted the shadow of a squirrel on the snow, moving almost parallel to us and just ahead, going the same direction we were.

"Must be a squirrel above us," I said.

Jiminy looked at me. "What do you mean? There are no trees here in the middle of the meadow. You talking about a *flying* squirrel?"

"No," I said. "Look, right there. See the shadow?" I pointed a ways in front of his head.

"Oh yeah. I didn't see it before."

We stopped and he made his point again. "I don't

know where that shadow of a squirrel is coming from," he said. "There's nothing above us, no trees, no poles, no power lines."

"How can that be?" I said.

"I have no idea," Jiminy answered. "When Ricky Potts told us about the shortcut, didn't he say folks call it *the valley of the shadow* or *shadow meadow* or something?"

"Yeah, something like that," I said. "Something about shadows. But even so, shadows don't exist on their own."

When we looked at the crusty snow in front of us, the squirrel's shadow was gone. Perhaps the squirrel had scampered off, taking its shadow with it. Then the shadow of a bird appeared almost where the squirrel had been, on the snow, as if there were one soaring high above us—*except there was nothing soaring above.* The only thing that seemed to be soaring—it had to be an illusion—was a bird's shadow on the snow that lay ahead of us.

"Jim," I said. "What do you make of this?"

"I don't know," he said. "It's awful strange. Maybe the meadow is haunted. I think we better get across it as quick as we can, and get out of here."

What lay ahead of us was snow on top of crustier snow that had iced over, so it was a little slick and we couldn't make good time. More and more shadows appeared in front of us and around us—what looked like the shadows of raccoons, possums, many other birds, and several squirrels.

"Is this starting to scare you?" Jiminy said. "It's like roadkill heaven. And even though I know they're only shadows, it's got me spooked. You scared?"

"I don't know as I'd say I'm scared," I said. "I suppose I'm like you—a little spooked." And then I thought to myself, *I'm not scared. I should be scared, but I'm not. Everything about this situation tells me to be scared, and yet I don't really have a lot of feelings about it—except maybe curiosity.*

We kept moving ahead, and more and more shadows, not connected to anything, apparently not made by anything, moved across the meadow, all around us. Ahead we could see the small cluster of trees that marked the end of the meadow.

Suddenly I did feel scared, and I didn't know why.

"I can't wait to get out of this creepy meadow now," I said. "Let's get to the other side."

"That's funny," Jim said. "I'm actually feeling calmer, almost relaxed enough to go to sleep."

"Like in the Wizard of Oz, right, when they crossed the poppy field?" I said, feeling as if everything was slowing down for me, too. I felt a chill up my backbone as I thought about it. Something was wrong, but I couldn't put my finger on it.

As we got within fifty yards of the trees somebody appeared, walking right toward us. He wasn't much bigger than Jiminy, maybe an inch or two taller, and by the way he walked we could tell he was a boy. Nothing about him was distinct. He looked like all the other shadows had except he had slight shades of color; he wasn't just black and white. He looked like he had a uniform on, perhaps one that was bluish-gray, with a little cap on his head that had a bill to it; the cap reminded me of a picture I'd once seen once of a train conductor in the old days.

"I've got a feeling," Jiminy said. "This is that Revolutionary War drummer boy we heard about."

And sure enough, when the shadowy figure got within ten feet of us, we stopped. I could see, even though it wasn't clear, that it was a ghost we were talking to. He stopped, too, and appeared to be looking at us, although we couldn't see eyes clearly on the shadowy figure.

"Welcome," a voice said. "It's good to have company."

I looked at Jiminy and Jiminy looked back at me. I thought my eyesight was beginning to go on me, because it was if I was looking at Jiminy through a light fog or a smoky haze, yet here he was no more than three feet from me.

"It's a strange meadow," I said to the drummer boy. "As we crossed it we saw shadows, but we didn't see what was making the shadows."

"Yes," the boy said, but I couldn't see any moving mouth. "That's all you'll find here—shadows."

When the drummer boy said that, Jiminy kind of laughed, as if the idea was preposterous. "Well, we're here, and we ain't shadows."

"Look again," the boy said.

I glanced again at Jiminy. His outline was less distinct than what I had seen a moment before. His colors, his clothing, his body, all his coloration had faded to half its brightness.

I looked at myself, my own colors were fading—not as fast as Jiminy's—but mine were half as dull as his. Something was dreadfully wrong.

"Before long," the drummer boy said, "You'll be like me."

"But why?" I cried.

"How?" Jiminy said.

"Don't you understand?" the drummer boy said. "The animals died. Their shadows are all that's left."

"What are you saying?" I said. "Are you a ghost? Or a shadow?"

"I'm not sure," the drummer boy said. "Perhaps one or the other, or both. I was killed in this meadow by a musket ball long ago. It seems like yesterday, but it was long ago in your understanding of time."

"So what about us?" Jiminy said. "We're not dead. We haven't been killed."

I glanced at Jim and saw he had faded more. I could barely make out any clarity, the color of his eyes or even the sharpness of the iris. I looked down at myself. I hadn't changed much since my last look.

"It was the trucks, the semis, wasn't it?" Jiminy said, and the drummer boy shrugged what had once been his shoulders.

"I don't know," he said. "I wasn't there. I was here in the meadow. What happened to you must have happened just before the meadow, close by."

"We've got to get out of here," I said, and touched Jim on the arm. My hand went through what should have been the substance of it. "Come on, Jim. We need to go now!"

Jim started moving forward, toward the trees.

"Not that way," I said. "Back."

I turned, but my body felt heavy as a log and my movement was slow-motion, as if I was trying to run in chest-high water. It took every ounce of strength I had to go in the direction we had come from.

"Jim," I gasped. "Come on. Let's go."

But I heard nothing from him, and something told me I couldn't afford to turn and call him again. So I forced my way forward—backward, actually, backward toward the opening in the trees where we had entered the meadow. As I did, everything seemed to be like a movie running backward. I saw the shadows of the raccoons and the squirrels and the birds moving in reverse, as if time and motion were going backwards as I reversed the distance. It took me I don't know how long—hours, it seemed—until finally I made it to the edge of the woods. I stepped over what felt to me like a boundary, a line almost like the starting line at a track meet or the finish line at a marathon, except it was more than that; it was an energy boundary, a life-force boundary. When my feet hit the other side of that line, I felt myself grabbed by some sort of a huge suctioning force, a gravitational pull that yanked me back at the speed of light.

After that, I have no idea what happened until I felt the pain of light as I opened my eyes in what turned out to be a hospital room. A nurse was there, and my mother and my sister. My mother and my sister began crying and hugging me. I ached all over and somehow knew my legs were both broken.

"Where am I?" I remember saying.

The words tumbled out of their mouths, telling me I had been in a terrible accident, I had been run over by a tractor-trailer on the highway. The truck driver had seen me skid and fall and slide under him on the black ice. I'd been in a coma for four days. My survival had been touch and go.

"Where's Jim?" I said. "What about Jim?"

My mother's and sister's eyes told the story. Jim hadn't made it. I sobbed.

Three months later, when I was up to it, and after I had told my mother and sister about the meadow, the three of us went there. We didn't come in from the highway side; there was no place to park. Instead we came in from the side I had never reached, the side with the small clump of trees, near where we had seen the drummer boy and where I had last seen Jim. We walked around the meadow, which had no snow on it now. The grass was beginning to sprout, it was spring-time, and everything was coming alive again. There were buds on the trees and the sap was flowing freely. There were no shadows like I had seen with Jim. The only shadows we saw now were the normal shadows one would expect to see: the shadows at the base of a tree, extending out from its foot, the shadow of a gull or a hawk on the ground before us, and the gull or the hawk circling above us between the ground and the sun. Everything was normal, and I thought what a great place it would be to establish a park.

"Maybe you could just leave me alone here for a minute," I said, standing in the center of the meadow.

My mother and sister moved off and stood talking quietly near where we had come in.

I closed my eyes, trying to recall my friend Jimmy Critchlow's face. But it wouldn't come to me. I concentrated harder. Nothing. Finally I opened my eyes, and just then a cloud passed overhead, blocking the sun.

In front of me I saw three shadows, the closest—my own—stretching before me, feet touching my feet. The others—two boys who didn't get to become men—lay flat ten feet away. One held out his arms to me, the other carried a drum on his hip. With the sun behind the cloud I felt a chill on the back of my neck—or was it more? My arms felt as if they were being pulled toward the two shadows by a magnet. On the ground before me I could see the arms of my shadow quivering, trying to rise. I struggled to keep my own arms at my side, though they fought to rise. Were Jim and the drummer boy trying to pull me across? Had I cheated death that day we took the shortcut? The meadow had a hold on me right then, and even though I thought I was physically stronger this time, I wasn't sure I could resist the way I had the day of the accident.

"Ben!" a voice called. It was my mother. "Ben, time to go home."

I stood frozen to the spot, and despite the coolness of the air now, I could feel the sweat of exertion breaking out on my forehead. I was losing the battle, my arms were gradually rising, following the urging of my shadow arms. I was being drawn somewhere. Where, I didn't know.

"Honey, are you ready to go?" Mom said from right behind me.

I felt her hand on my arm, then another hand, my sister's. Their added weight seemed to break the spell. My arms relaxed and I had control over my body again.

A moment later the cloud passed and the sun warmed me again. The two shadows vanished, leaving only mine, my mother's and my sister's. We turned and walked out of the meadow.

For years my eighth-grade best-friend Jiminy Cricket visited me in my dreams, always beckoning me to explore some shortcut with him or depart on some grand adventure. I successfully resisted time and time again—saying no or walking away or offering an excuse—so that eventually his appearances in my dreams diminished and then stopped. But he'll be back, Jiminy will. I know he'll return. And someday my shadowy friend will extend those arms to me and I'll relax and go.

But not yet.

THE FRENCH ACRE

DEVANEY TOOK THE PHONE CALL about the crows. It was Fourth of July weekend. My wife Carol and her mother were off at church and I was relaxing on my new redwood chaise lounge with a mug of French Roast and the Sunday funnies. My father-in-law Devaney, whom Carol and her mother called my part-ner-in-crime, came back from the living room with the portable phone in his hand. He set it on the end table between us and plopped heavily onto his patio chair.

"I'll leave it out here," he said. "That way we won't have to run in and get it every time it rings."

I tried to go back to reading *Hagar the Horrible*, but Devaney interrupted before I could start it.

"Don't you want to know who that was?" he said.

I didn't look up, but out of the corner of my eye I could see him scratching with his pen in his little note-book, playing cat-and-mouse with me. This was exact-ly why my mother-in-law appreciated me—I kept her retired-history-teacher husband out of her hair. But I had to admit, he wasn't always annoying, and he was a pretty fair amateur shutterbug. He had shot some darned good photos to accompany the feature stories I wrote for the *Valley News*, the daily that serves the small Vermont and New Hampshire towns within a forty-mile radius of White River Junction.

"Is there a story in it or not?" I said, trying not to look up. But I couldn't keep my mind on Hagar. I looked up.

Devaney smiled, a big cat-ate-the-canary smile.

"Remember *The Birds*?" he said. "Hitchcock? Suzanne Pleshette? Rod Steiger? Peck, peck, peck?"

I nodded. "It was Rod Taylor, not Rod *Steiger.* What about it?"

"Not *it*!" he said. "Not *it*! *They*! *The birds*! They're here!" He made his eyes go as wide as they could, then puckered his lips and began whistling the *Twilight Zone* theme song.

Ever since we'd investigated Norwich's humming church bell and the Witness Tree on the green, people had been phoning us—me and Devaney instead of the police—when something a little out-of-the-ordinary came up. A cow couldn't just get lost; it disappeared, maybe got beamed up. So they phoned us. And a day or two after we met with the person calling it in, the cow would wander home or be found by a neighbor.

Or the lights in a Florida snowbird's house mysteriously came on and went off at odd hours, with no burglars to be seen anywhere near the place—so someone speculated that maybe ghosts were afoot in the haunted house. Devaney and I in turn called the snowbirds in Florida and learned that the lights were on automatic timers—but these were on a special irregular timer so burglars wouldn't easily spot a nightly pattern.

Sure, there were several other truly odd cases, but most of the calls were petty. Nevertheless people kept calling me and Devaney, as if we were the Upper Valley's sleuths of the paranormal or psychic detectives or something.

"Okay, which Looney Toon called this time?" I said.

"Nelda Potter. In Norwich. Remember Zack Potter? Used to have that farm stand beyond the curves on the way up to Beaver Meadow—that place where we got the pumpkins ten, fifteen years ago?"

"The dairy that became a Christmas tree farm?" I said, and Devaney nodded. "But Zack died."

"Of course he did," Devaney said with a scowl. "I know that. But she didn't. She's the one who called. I was just dropping his name to help orient you." Devaney rolled his eyes.

"Fine," I said, annoyed. "So Nelda Potter—Zack Potter's widow—called. Is she holed up in her house with swarms of starlings pecking through her wooden storm doors and shuttered windows? Rather than call 911, she chose to call the Psychic Detectives Hotline, right?"

"Closer to the truth than you think," Devaney said. "But it's not starlings. It's crows—hundreds of them."

"And?" No story I could pick out so far.

"And they're not attacking her house. They're roosting on that high wall around the French Acre."

Still no story that I could see. "You have a punch line to this?"

"Yes, I do." He paused for effect. "Nelda says there's never been a crow on those walls before, not ever. Birds won't go near it."

I looked at my father-in-law blankly.

"She says the crows showed up when Charlie Rivers started clearing the French Acre two weeks ago."

The French Acre was a walled-in acre of land whose overgrown interior was reported to be an almost impregnable thicket of bushes and trees. Legend had it that before the Revolutionary War the acre of pasture-land had been bounded by a waist-high stonewall. But something happened and the Norwich townsfolk added rocks and mortar, raising the wall's height to nine feet. Oddly, they left no gate and no door.

"You mean clearing brush around the *outside*, right?" I said. "*Outside* the walls, like cleaning up after the accident?"

Devaney and I had been at the French Acre two weeks earlier to cover the story at an accident scene. I'm a garden-variety reporter, a generalist, not an investigative reporter. Most of my stories are about high school graduations, charity cow-flop drops, 100th birthdays in nursing homes—local interest stuff, features, human interest pieces. But when the editors were shorthanded, my stories included the occasional accident.

Four teenage boys in a pickup—all four packed in across the front with no seatbelts—had died when they slammed into the wall at the French Acre. The impact punched a small hole in it, and I remembered someone at the scene trying to shine a flashlight in. *Holy mackerel*, the guy had said. *The brambles and trees are so thick in there you couldn't swing a hatchet.*

"No," Devaney said, bringing me back. "Nelda said he wasn't clearing brush outside; Charlie Rivers was clearing it *inside*, inside the French Acre."

I felt the short hairs on the back of my neck stand up.

"What time'd you tell Nelda we'd be out?"

"One o'clock."

"Call her back," I said. "And get your camera. Tell her we're on our way."

We passed Dan & Whit's Country Store, turned left at the Norwich Inn, and headed out the back road toward Beaver Meadow. Nelda Potter's farmhouse was only two or three minutes from the Inn, and the French Acre was along the way. I wanted to catch a glimpse of it in daylight. The last time I'd seen it, the night of the accident, its walls had been bathed in the light of emergency vehicles.

"Holy crow!" Devaney said as the walls of the French Acre came into view. "Pun intended."

Nelda Potter had been right. The high wall around it was rimmed with crows, hundreds of them. I pulled the car onto the dirt shoulder and we sat watching and listening.

"Notice anything?" I said after a minute or two.

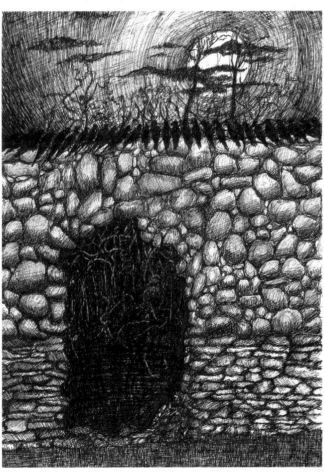

"Yeah," Devaney said. "They're quiet."

The lack of noise wasn't what I'd been getting at. But he was right. The crows weren't cawing. Not a single one of them. And they were all facing inward, looking down from their perches *into* the Acre, watching. Devaney pointed his camera and took a couple of shots of the birds.

"No. Look. The hole in the wall is bigger now," I said. "And there are brush piles along the outside, stuff that's been cleared out."

Devaney snapped another shot or two, this time of an opening that looked like an arched doorway to a ruined Scottish castle.

Just then a small blue pickup with a utility trailer pulled around us and stopped in front of the opening. A wiry older man got out, eyed us without waving, and began loading brush into the bed of the pickup and onto the utility trailer. His long gray hair was tied back in a ponytail. He didn't bother to shoo the crows.

"Charlie Rivers?" I said to Devaney.

"Looks like him. Want to talk to him now?"

"No, not yet. Nelda's waiting," I said, starting the car. "Besides, when we come back this way, Charlie should be loaded up and gone. If he is, we can take a look inside for ourselves."

"And I can shoot some pictures."

We gave Rivers a polite New England nod and a wave as we eased onto the road. The man in the blue jeans and chamois shirt nodded and went back to work.

Nelda Potter's white-clapboarded farmhouse sat on the opposite side of the road, less than a half mile beyond the French Acre. She waved from her porch rocker as we pulled into the driveway. Five minutes later we were in her parlor with teacups on our laps.

"So, tell us about the crows, Mrs. Potter," I said.

"And what you know about the French Acre."

"Well," she started. "There's been a lot of deaths there."

"Four," I said. "Teenage boys. A terrible waste. We covered the story for the *Valley News*."

"Besides those four, I mean. There's been ten or a dozen over the years. I remember young Henry Corbett in the 1950s. The Tucker girl and her boyfriend in '63. Mary Grady's twin boys from up the road, around '67, they crashed on Graduation night. Then others in the seventies, eighties, nineties. It's a bad spot—and there's not even a curve there; that's what I don't get. They just wind it up on the straightaway and hit that damned wall—pardon my French."

"And the birds?" Devaney said. "You said there have never been birds on the wall of the French Acre?"

"Mr. Devaney, Mr. Hoag, I'm eighty years old. I've lived on this farm for sixty of those years, and my husband lived here all of his seventy-eight. His family went back seven generations here. Everybody on this road knows that no crows—no birds of any type, not a robin or a sparrow—go near that cursed acre. There's been nothing live there except trees and brush that have grown up inside and died and rotted there, then grown up again. There's something wrong with it."

"Any idea what?" I said.

"Well, they call it the French Acre, supposedly— Mr. Devaney, as a former history teacher you may know this—because a contingent of Lafayette's soldiers camped there just before or during the American Revolution, 1774 or 1776, sometime thereabouts. It was a pasture then, with a low stonewall around it. At least that's the way I've always heard it—Lafayette's soldiers."

"But something happened," Devaney interrupted.

"Yes," she said. "They died. All of them. It's the *how*

that's a mystery. But whatever happened, people felt the need to wall up the Acre."

The three of us sat quiet a minute.

"I'd heard this before," Devaney said. "There's speculation it was disease. Or bad food or poison water."

"But why build a nine foot wall around it?" I said. "With no plaque or historical marker. Did they die overnight? Or was it over several weeks or months? Was it a quarantine situation? Is that why they built the wall? There's got to be something written down somewhere. Town records. An old diary. Something other than word of mouth."

"And what's it got to do with crows?" Devaney said.

"I don't know," Nelda Potter said with a shrug. "What's it got to do with Mr. Rivers?"

Devaney and I looked at each other, then back at Nelda.

"Who hired him?" I asked. "To clear out the brush."

"I have no idea," she said. "Maybe the Town? As far as I know, there's no Society or Association that looks over the site, not like a cemetery association or historical society. Nobody's ever tended it."

"Maybe the families of the boys who were killed hired him," Devaney said. "Or their insurance companies?" But that didn't make sense.

"So why is Charlie Rivers down there bush-hogging it out?" I said to Nelda. "He must have been hired because he's a handyman, a yard cleanup guy, right?"

"I have no idea," she said. "I've talked with all my neighbors on the road and nobody seems to know who'd hire him for it, or why."

"And what do you know about Charlie Rivers?" I asked.

"Well, he lives a few miles north of here, past the Beaver Meadow Chapel where the road goes from paved to dirt at the Norwich/Sharon line. He's always been quiet. He's in his seventies, eight or ten years younger than I am. He's part Abenaki Indian—name's actually Charlie Three Rivers. Worked a bunch of different jobs over the years, including helping me and my husband in haying season, but mostly he makes his living mowing cemeteries in Norwich and Sharon. If you need to know more, you could check with Dutch Roberts, the Norwich town constable, and Oscar Bell, the Town Manager up to Sharon."

After we said our goodbyes to Nelda Potter, we drove back to the French Acre and pulled off the road. No sign of Charlie Rivers or his truck. We got out and stood in front of the newly enlarged breach in the wall.

"It's dark in there," Devaney said, snapping a picture. "Like a cave."

I stepped through the opening and almost fell forward. I caught my balance by putting a hand on the wall, and found myself standing ankle-deep in soil.

"You okay, Hoag?" Devaney called from behind me. He shone his flashlight in.

"I'm fine. But watch your step. It's soft. I think it's silt and loam from years and years of rotting vegetation."

"Geez," Devaney said, stepping in behind me. "You can hardly see the sky in here. It's really thick overhead. Charlie Rivers has barely made a dent in it."

He was right, Charlie Rivers hadn't cleared a hundredth of it yet. But he'd begun. The word *thicket* came to mind. What was left was an impenetrable woven thicket. I doubted anyone could successfully crawl from one wall of the French Acre to its opposite wall.

"So, what do we see?" Devaney said. He handed me his flashlight and I did a quick search.

"Nothing out of the ordinary," I said. "You see anything from back there?"

"Nope. You've got my flashlight."

"Hear anything?"

"Nope. Not even the crows."

"Smell or taste anything?" I asked.

Devaney said nothing for a moment, and I thought maybe he hadn't heard my question. Then he answered. "Death, I think."

"You mean like rotting leaves?" I said.

I shut up and breathed it in through my nose. Yes, it was layer upon layer of rotting vegetation. But it was also something hard to pinpoint. Devaney was right. Whatever it was, the smell made the word *death* appear in one's mind. And it gave me goosebumps.

"It is death," came a voice from behind, startling us. We turned toward the light of the doorway. A thin man's shadowy profile leaned on the wall.

"Charlie Rivers," Devaney said. "Didn't hear you sneak up."

"Didn't sneak," the man said. "I parked the truck by your car and walked over to look inside. Tried my best to not scare you."

"The Acre's scary enough," I said. "Especially the inside of it."

"Oh, it's not so bad once you get used to it. Would you prefer to come outside in the light and talk? I figure you've got questions. And you can empty your shoes out, so you don't track it all over your wife's carpet."

We stepped out.

"Devaney and Hoag," I said, and the three of us shook hands.

"*Valley News,*" Rivers said. "I've read your stuff. Especially liked that piece on the Norwich Witch a couple years back."

Rivers was friendlier and more outgoing than I'd expected. He dropped the tailboard of his utility trailer and extended an open hand. Devaney and I sat down. Rivers stood.

"We got a call about the crows," I said. "The caller said it's the first time a bird or beast has come near the French Acre. Is that true?"

"Could be," Rivers said. "I don't keep watch over every little thing along this road like some of the busybodies do. But still, there's a ring of truth to it."

"So what's your part in it?" Devaney asked. "Somebody hire you to clear it out?"

"Nope," Rivers said, looking down at the ground. "Nobody's paying me. And nobody asked me to do it."

"Then why?" Devaney asked.

"It couldn't be put off any longer, not after those four boys. And that's when it opened up."

"Opened up?" Devaney said.

Rivers motioned toward the new entrance through the wall.

"I've got to take care of it before someone else is killed here," he said. "It's just something I've got to do."

"If you're intending to clear that entire Acre, it'll take you a year," I said. With only that one small opening you can't get in with a bulldozer or a backhoe or anything very mechanical."

"It's got to be done pretty much by hand, anyway," Rivers said. "You can't bulldoze." He looked up at me and said, "And no, I don't need help. It's something I've got to do alone."

"And just what is it you're attempting to do?" Devaney said. "Is it about the French soldiers, the ones who fell to the disease?"

"Who said anything about disease?" Rivers said, jumping down off the trailer. He grabbed an ax and a shovel and walked toward the opening. "Devaney, Hoag, nice to meet you. If you'll excuse me, I've got to get back to it if I'm to finish in less than a year."

After the holiday weekend Devaney and I visited Dutch Roberts, Norwich's town constable, at his office. We'd known each other awhile and he'd always been helpful when I needed information for a story.

"Charlie Rivers has been the groundskeeper for three or four of our smaller Norwich cemeteries for about thirty years now," Dutch said. "He mows and trims, fills in graves that have settled, resets the stones that tip or fall, that kind of thing. Does the same thing for Town of Sharon at two or three of theirs. Put it all together and he makes a basic living part of the year."

"What's he do the rest of the year? Go to Florida?" Devaney asked, chuckling.

"I think he hauls firewood and plows snow. One winter he went to work for Henry Mason over at the funeral home."

"He's not trained or certified as a mortician's assistant, is he?" I said. "That'd take some basic education and licensing."

"Well, no," Dutch said. "Not quite at that level. Not assisting with embalming or anything. Charlie was more of a fill-in to help wheel in the bodies and open doors at wakes and help with funeral parking."

"Does he still do it?" I asked.

"Nah. That was six or eight years ago. Henry let him go after a month. Charlie told him he was getting vibes from the stiffs."

A half hour later we were in Sharon, chatting across the desk with Oscar Bell, the Town Manager.

"A reliable worker, Charlie is. Been taking care of four of our cemeteries for years. He even found one up in Beaver Meadow, a cemetery we didn't even know about. It was terribly overgrown, neglected for a hundred years. No idea how he located it. It wasn't until he'd cleared it all out that we even found it on one of the old maps."

"You know anything about his history—like his family, education, jobs?" Devaney asked.

Devaney knew we shouldn't be asking the question, and I knew it, too. What's more, Oscar Bell knew it. But he wasn't a stiff bureaucrat, he was also a friend. He went to a file cabinet, slid open a drawer, and fanned his way through a sheaf of papers in a manila file.

"Pardon me while I think out loud," he said. "High school grad. Odd jobs. Never married. Supported his mother, one of the last of the Abenaki medicine women, who lived with him until she died about five years ago. That's about it." Oscar turned back to face us.

"Sounds like Charlie Rivers you're talking about," said a voice from the doorway. Devaney and I turned in our chairs and saw a bent-over old man leaning on a cane.

"Well, I'll be damned. Alton Brock," Devaney said, rising to greet the man with a handshake and a slap on the shoulder. "Come in, come in, my old friend. Hoag, you remember Alton Brock, don't you, the unofficial mayor of Sharon, the man who single-handedly raised the money for the new school?"

I nodded, shook hands, and Devaney motioned Alton Brock toward a chair.

"Oh, I can't stay, Devaney," Brock said. "I've got a meeting down the hall. But I couldn't help overhearing you three when I was walking by."

"You know Charlie Rivers?" I asked. "From some cemetery association meeting, right?"

"Oh, I know him," Brock said. "But not from that. Many of the old-timers here in Sharon know him—*if they're drinking water.* When he was young—I doubt he's done it in forty years or more—Charlie Rivers was the best apple-branch dowser around. If you needed a well, you called Charlie. He could locate water with a divining rod in places you'd never believe you'd find it. And he was always right. Never saw him fail. Charlie Rivers had The Sense."

"The Sense?" I said.

"Well, sure," Brock continued. "You know, the sensitivity. Not everybody can do it. It's a combination of the apple-branch and The Sense. My mother—God rest her soul—told me it was like mind-reading the earth. That's what Charlie Rivers could do."

I had a restful evening at home that night, because there was no story to write. It just wasn't there. Instead I made notes about what I knew so far. And I asked Devaney to do a little research on the French Acre, Lafayette's troops, and what else was going on around Norwich around the time of the Revolution. Then I called Nelda Potter back to get the names of the accident victims she'd spieled off. It wouldn't be difficult to check the Norwich Town cops and the State Police for accident reports connected to the French Acre over the last forty years.

Two days later Devaney called to say he'd hit a dead end. In fact, he found no evidence of French soldiers being in the area before or during the Revolution.

"I checked Dartmouth's library with a fine-toothed comb," he said. "Despite the spot being called the French Acre, there's nothing to support the idea that French soldiers came anywhere near Norwich. Several British contingents passed through and likely camped here, but no French."

It took me two weeks to find and go through all the Town and State accidents reports. Eleven people had been killed at the French Acre since 1935. They had all been coming from the same direction at a high rate of speed and, based on the sketches and photos in the files, the vehicles had all impacted the wall in practically the same spot.

When I told Devaney what I'd found in the reports, he looked pensive.

"Were there also accidents *without* fatalities?" he said. "I mean that's a lot of deaths. Didn't anybody ever walk away from one?"

"Nope."

He was right. Not a fender-bender in the bunch. No one with a broken arm or leg, no one ever hospitalized.

"All fatalities," I said. "What are the odds?"

"The wall's like a death magnet."

I had enough background material to do a first story on the French Acre, a curiosity story. But because of the recent accident resulting in the four boys' deaths, I decided against it. A curiosity piece could wait. No matter when it saw print, it would reopen old wounds, but right now the wounds were too fresh. I let it rest awhile.

The leaves were starting to turn—golds and early reds—when we drove to the French Acre to see Charlie Rivers again. Hills of dead and dying brush had begun to pile up outside the wall. Charlie's truck and trailer were nowhere in sight. Hundreds of crows perched on the wall.

"Looks like he's given up hauling it to the landfill," I said.

"Maybe he wants to spend all his time and energy clearing," Devaney said.

We stepped through the opening in the wall.

"Hey, Charlie, you in there?" I called, not expecting to find him. We were amazed to see the progress Rivers had made.

"Wow," Devaney said. "He's really gaining ground."

"Literally and figuratively," I said. In the five weeks since the crash he'd cleared a quarter acre.

"What's that?" Devaney said, pointing.

"A chainsaw," I said.

"No, not that. *That. Those.*"

Before I could answer, Devaney had his camera in front of his broad face and was snapping pictures. In front of us were reflectors, red ones on aluminum rods, the sort you'd see marking the edge of a driveway. There were seven.

"What do you think they're there for?" I said.

"No idea," Devaney said. "A couple are close together, but then there's one way over there, another out that way. And nothing connecting them, like string or crime scene tape. I don't know, Hoag. Bodies, you think?"

"Maybe. If there really are bodies here. If there are, how would he know where they are?"

"He has The Sense," Devaney said. "And didn't Oscar tell us the man's a dowser?"

"A dowser, yes. But a dowser of the dead?"

We heard the crunch of gravel along the road, then the sputtering sound of an engine that didn't want to shut off. We stepped back out into the full daylight.

"Hello, Hoag, Devaney," Charlie Rivers said.

"Hi, Charlie," I said. "You're making great progress, I see. That's damned backbreaking work. You're twice the man I am. I don't have the stamina for it at my age."

"And I sure don't," Devaney said with a laugh.

Charlie reached into the back of his pickup and pulled out a handful of the red reflectors on aluminum rods.

"Those things help you keep your bearings in there?" Devaney said.

"Gotta use 'em," Charlie Rivers said. "Nobody else knows where they are."

"The bodies?" I said. "Of the French soldiers?"

Charlie moved toward the opening. "After all these years I wouldn't say *bodies*."

"Bones, then," Devaney said. "*Bones* of the French soldiers?"

Charlie paused at the opening, smiled quizzically and said, "Who said they were French?" He ducked his head inside and stepped through. "Excuse me, gentlemen. I've got to get back to work now. Deadlines, you know, something newspapermen should understand." And he disappeared inside.

Devaney called, "Are you saying they *weren't* French?"

"Do your own homework."

It was Monday of Columbus Day weekend and the foliage was at its peak when Devaney called me.

"You on a car phone?" I said. "You sound funny."

"One of those new cellular phones," he said. "It's my cousin Bernie's."

"Bernie's? You're in Connecticut? Or is Bernie at your place?"

"We're in Connecticut. We came down for the long weekend."

"You didn't mention it to me. Carol and I didn't even know you were gone."

"Spur of the moment, I suppose. You know how I sometimes get inspiration. Well, yesterday the thought just jumped into my head—*call Bernie, call Bernie*. It wouldn't go away. So I called Bernie."

"And?"

"Bernie invites us to spend the long weekend. It's only a three-hour drive, so we pack a bag and head out the door. You know, I never do these last-minute things. But this just felt like the thing to do. To make a long story short, we arrived late last night and didn't have much time to chitchat before we turned in. But this morning Bernie and I are having breakfast and I mention what you and I are working on—you know, the French Acre—and Bernie says, 'Reminds me of the French soldiers buried in the Revolutionary War cemetery over at Norwich.' *Norwich*, Hoag. Norwich, *Connecticut*, he means. He tells me it's only a twenty minute drive, so here we are."

"Here we are? Where?"

"Norwich. Connecticut. The cemetery, Hoag. Aren't you listening, son? Bernie and I are standing in the cemetery in Norwich, Connecticut. I'm looking at a stone, a memorial to twenty of Lafayette's French soldiers who died in camp here in 1778. *It's Norwich, Connecticut, not Norwich, Vermont.* Someplace along the way, I think, this story got mixed in with ours."

"Get a picture of the stone, Devaney," I said. "I'll see you when you get back." I hung up and drove straight for the French Acre.

From a half mile away I could see Charlie Rivers' truck. I eased over onto the shoulder a distance away, then walked the last hundred yards. When I poked my head in the hole in the wall, Charlie was standing near the most recently cleared section, facing away from me. He held a small split branch in his hands. I stood perfectly still and watched.

"No sense gawking, whoever you are," he called, not turning around. "Come in, if you like."

"It's Hoag," I said, stepping in on the silty floor of what had become a third-of-an-acre room without a ceiling.

"No Devaney? He sick?"

"Guess you're not clairvoyant after all," I said. "He's away for the long weekend." I labored through the soft soil toward Rivers.

"Okay, Devaney's away. What brings you out?"

Rivers said, turning. "It's a lovely day, a long weekend, you should be enjoying yourself, Hoag, maybe doing a little leaf-peeping."

"What brings me out is the soldiers. Devaney did his homework. You were right. They're not French soldiers. That story comes from a different Norwich, the one in Connecticut. Somehow the story of Lafayette's soldiers dying of disease while encamped at a place called Norwich got mixed in, or borrowed, or co-opted, whatever, with something similar here. Right? What we call the French Acre isn't French at all, is it?"

"Nope. It's British."

"British? How do you know that? This whole walled-in crypt may be just another Cardiff Giant, a colossal hoax. We've found nothing written down anywhere that would suggest *anything* actually happened to a detachment of French, American, British, German, or other soldiers here—or to anyone, for that matter. Maybe it was just a cow pasture. If something happened, don't you think someone would have recorded it?"

"I'm pretty sure I've located thirteen so far," Rivers said, motioning toward the reflectors.

A little leap in the pit of my stomach told me he was right.

"There was a reason no one ever wrote it down," he said.

He was forcing my brain to work hard now.

"Shame?" I said. "Something they didn't want future generations to know about?"

Charlie nodded.

"Like maybe the soldiers were sick and quarantined," I said. "But the Colonists abandoned them—and walled them in?"

Charlie Rivers said nothing, and I stood mulling it over in my reporter's mind.

"Then if none of this is written down," I said, "how did you know?"

"Oral history. Indian. My mother was an Abenaki medicine woman. She passed the story on to me. She said the whites wouldn't tell it, wanted to forget it." Rivers sat on a stump and motioned for me to sit on a log.

"They did not die of disease, my mother said. Shortly after the American Revolution began, twenty of the King's soldiers camped here in the pasture. The men of Norwich who were able-bodied enough to fight had already left to join the armies of the Colonies, so the few males who were left were either young or old or infirm. It was largely a community of women."

"Are you saying the soldiers went into town and raped them?" I said, thinking I could see where he was going.

"No, they didn't," Rivers said. "In fact, if they had, what followed might have seemed somehow justified. But the soldiers were gentlemen. They hired six women to cook for them here at the pasture campsite. But the women feared their militiamen husbands might meet these same British soldiers on the battlefield. So they obtained a sleeping potion and mixed it with the soldiers' evening meal. While the twenty soldiers slept soundly, the women slit their throats, all twenty of them. They hastily buried the dead where they had bled out."

"But why the wall?" I said. "To hide the shame?"

"Maybe," Rivers said.

"What're you thinking?" I said. "That the wall was to keep the spirits in?"

Rivers shrugged. "I don't know. They're here, though."

"And you think that's what's caused the crashes, the deaths?" I said. "Every one a fatality, never a survivor. You think the spirits inside—on the desecrated ground—drew the vehicles and passengers to the wall?"

Rivers shrugged again, and I glanced at the reflectors.

"So what's your part in all this? What drew you in?"

"The last accident with the four boys. That one finally opened a hole in the wall. For years I sensed something here, but I couldn't tell exactly what. The morning after this accident, when I stood by the break in the wall, I knew what I had to do."

"Mark the graves?" I said.

Rivers didn't answer at first, looked away from me. Then he said, "Yeah, mark the graves."

"You believe that'll make the difference?" I said. "You think it'll stop the accidents? I mean, wouldn't it be easier to just press the Town to tear down the wall?"

"Crazy as it sounds, it's a historic site," Rivers said. "The parents of the last two kids killed here tried to have it demolished and failed. Anyway, it's a part of people's mental landscape. Too much public sentiment in favor of keeping it."

"But back to my question," I said. "Do you somehow believe dowsing the dead and putting up grave markers will put an end to it?"

Rivers mistook my impatience, my reporter-style interrogation, for hostility.

"Excuse me," he said, rising to his feet. "I've got at least a half acre left to clear and time's running out."

He picked up the chainsaw and fired it up, but even at the eruption of the saw the necklace of crows on the wall never flinched.

When Devaney got back from Connecticut, I filled him in on my visit with Charlie Rivers.

"What do you suppose he means, *time's running out*?" Devaney said.

"I assume he means time's running out to get the brush cleared and the spots marked."

"But what's this time limit he's up against?" Devaney said. "Does he have to finish before the snow flies? Before the year is out? Before Halloween and the witching hour?"

"Maybe before the wall claims any more victims," I said.

"Oh, come on, Hoag, we aren't buying into that yet, are we? As far as I can see, what we've got is a string of unrelated automobile accidents over a period of decades, an old dowser clearing brush, and thirteen driveway reflectors that might—*might*—be marking some Revolutionary War graves. Heck, you haven't even got enough to pull together a story on it yet, have you?"

Something Devaney said struck me—*a string of unrelated automobile accidents.*

"They're not unrelated automobile accidents," I said. "They're all related to the French Acre. And they all resulted in fatalities, no survivors. There's something here, Devaney. I know there's something here, and it's got to do with Charlie Rivers' story."

"Don't forget the crows," Devaney. "I don't suppose you asked Rivers about the crows."

I hadn't. I'd completely forgotten.

"Tell you what, Devaney," I said. "This week you do a little genealogical research."

"On who? Or is it *whom*?" he said, rolling his eyes.

"On the car crash victims."

"The four boys?"

"No. On all of them. See if they trace back to Colonial families who lived in Norwich."

"What? What are you thinking, Hoag—that it's a revenge thing, the march of the dead soldiers?"

"I don't know what it is. But if there are ties here—if they're all descendants of the women who massacred those British soldiers—there's enough for a story."

"And what're you gonna do?"

"I'm going out to help Charlie Rivers."

"Help him do what?"

"Clear brush," I said. "And dowse the dead."

For the next three weeks I worked side-by-side with Charlie Rivers. He didn't talk much, and I didn't pressure him. A nominal trust seemed to build between us—or maybe he was simply ignoring me. On my fifth day I noticed several new reflectors in the ground. He must have dowsed at night or before I arrived that morning. Another reflector appeared the tenth day, giving a total of seventeen. That's what we had on Halloween morning, October 31. We also still had a quarter acre of brush to clear.

"Hoag," Charlie said that day as we sat eating lunch from paper bags. "I appreciate your help. I really do."

"Are you disappointed we won't get it cleared by tonight?" I said, remembering Devaney's comment about Halloween and the witching hour.

"No. Why?" Rivers said, looking surprised.

"Oh, I don't know," I said. "I just thought, you know, Halloween, the crows, the deadline you mentioned."

"What about the crows?"

"Well, you never mention them. There are hundreds of them. They've been here for almost four months now. They wouldn't come near this place for decades, maybe longer. What do you make of them?"

"Harbingers of death, I suppose. Don't you think? I mean, most cultures see ravens and crows as symbols of death, right?"

"But the four kids died months ago. These soldiers—if they are indeed under this soil—died hundreds of years ago. Why are the crows still here?"

"You're the reporter, Hoag," Charlie Rivers said, and got to his feet. "I don't explain this stuff. I just sense it."

That afternoon, after we cleared a small patch of brush, Rivers let me watch as he used a split apple branch to dowse it. I'd never seen anyone dowse for water before—certainly never for bodies—and I had a healthy skepticism based on the ouija board I'd tried using with my cousins when we were kids. But when Charlie stood over a certain spot, the stick did seem to quiver faintly in his rough hands. He had me mark the location with a reflector.

I left early that afternoon to get home for trick-or-treaters. Charlie said he'd stay until dark.

Devaney's geneaology search didn't produce the results I had hoped for. Not one victim had a connection to any colonial Norwich families.

"But I did discover something else," Devaney said. "It looks like every one of them had a trace of Abenaki Indian blood in their veins."

The next day was Saturday. Devaney and I drove to the French Acre right after breakfast, both dressed to clear brush. The crows were there, but Charlie Rivers hadn't arrived. We poked our heads in, then stepped inside and nosed around.

Eighteen markers. Maybe an eighth of an acre left to clear.

"Guess All Saints Day isn't his deadline," I said. "That's today."

We heard a vehicle crunch up on the gravel. A minute later Dutch Roberts stepped into the mostly cleared French Acre. He gave a whistle of surprise.

"Morning, Hoag, Devaney," he said. "What brings you two out on a Saturday? Looks like you're dressed for gardening."

"We're giving Charlie a hand today," I said. "It's a lot of work for one man alone. And what about you? What brings you out? Come to help?"

"Hell, no," Dutch laughed. "Did enough bush-hogging when I was younger. My back won't stand it now. If I laid into it, I'd have to spend the afternoon on the heating pad."

I could see Dutch's eyes sweeping the place, taking in the reflectors.

"The graveyard's grown," he said.

"What makes you think it's a graveyard?" Devaney said.

We hadn't been in touch with Dutch since the week following the accident.

"Oh, just a guess," Dutch said. "Not very orderly rows, though. Maybe it'll all make more sense when you put up the little flags."

"What flags?" I said. Dutch looked genuinely surprised that we didn't know.

"The ones Charlie Rivers ordered through Dan and Whit's store. They're the size you put on graves for the holidays."

"How'd you find out?" I said.

"Oh, a bunch of us were shooting the breeze at Dan & Whit's. Veteran's Day came up, which is what—nine or ten days away? The store clerk mentions Charlie Rivers was in the other day and hit the roof because his two twelve-packs of flags hadn't come in. Seems he'd ordered them around Labor Day—a special order—and the clerk had forgotten to call it in. So now Charlie's sweating it. They told him they'd call around to flag stores and distributors."

"But what's the big deal?" Devaney said. "Charlie can go down to the VFW or the American Legion and get them, no problem."

"No you can't, Devaney," Dutch said. "They're foreign flags, not American flags. French, I'd guess. Makes sense, this being the French Acre. So I'm figuring the flags will take the place of the reflectors on Veteran's Day. Maybe Charlie will have a little memorial service."

I could see Devaney was itching to say, "Or maybe two dozen British Union Jacks," so I shot him a button-your-lip look. Although Rivers hadn't said the story he shared with me was told in confidence, I presumed it was, so I'd said nothing to anyone except Devaney, who had followed suit. And we didn't tell Dutch then.

Charlie Rivers still hadn't shown up by the time Dutch left, so Devaney and I worked for a couple of hours clearing brush, then drove to Dan and Whit's for coffee and sandwiches.

"We're helping Charlie clear brush down at the French Acre," I said. "I know he ordered some cemetery flags—French, maybe—and I wondered when they're expected in."

"British, not French," the clerk was quick to correct. "And they'll be here in under two weeks."

"So not in time for Veteran's Day next week?" Devaney said.

"No. But I asked Mr. Rivers about that, too. He said he didn't need them for Veteran's Day. He'll have them soon."

In the car Devaney said, "So if the deadline isn't Veteran's Day, when is it? And why?"

"I don't know," I said. "But I'm worried about Charlie. I'm going to call his house and see what's up."

Rivers sounded puny when he answered the

phone. He'd come down with the flu and was worried it would put him behind schedule. I said we'd drop by with some hot soup from Dan & Whit's.

Twenty minutes later we were in Charlie's living room. He lay on his couch, wrapped in a blanket, shivering. On the coffee table sat a jar of yellow powder, a blue bottle, and a bowl containing a bright yellow paste.

"Home remedies?" I said.

"Abenaki potions," he said. "For big aches and pains." He wasn't kidding. The man was sick. He looked terrible.

"Try an old-fashioned remedy from *our tribe*," Devaney said, holding out the container of chicken soup.

Charlie smiled weakly and said thanks. After an awkward silence he admitted he was worried about the French Acre, so I volunteered to keep working at it while he was down with the flu. He was grateful.

"Clear, but don't dig up anything, Hoag," he said. "Same as we've been doing it all along. Don't disturb what's under."

"Want us to try dowsing, too?" Devaney said. This was his first day working inside the French Acre.

"You're welcome to try," Rivers said. "I doubt you'll have much luck. If you haven't sensed water, you probably won't sense the dead. But who knows? It won't hurt to try. Even if you don't locate anyone, I'll be back soon."

We stood at Rivers' front door and I called back to him, "What's the deadline?"

"Umm, night of the twenty-fourth," he said. "It's got to be ready by then."

"Why the twenty-fourth?" Devaney said.

"You'll see," Rivers called back, then whispered loudly, comically, "It's a secret."

The next day was Sunday, so Devaney and I only put in half a day's work, a three-hour morning. We cleared a twenty-by-ten piece of land that each of us tried unsuccessfully to dowse. Maybe there just wasn't anybody down there. As we gathered our tools together to leave, the two of us stood in the center of what was essentially a huge, high-walled, private cemetery for a very few inhabitants.

"Notice something different, Devaney?" I said.

Devaney beamed proudly. "Yeah, it's just a little bit bigger now, Hoag, thanks to our efforts."

"No," I said. "Something else." He looked up and his body slowly made the turn.

"Damn," he said. "No crows. Not a single, damned crow. Were they around when we got here this morning?"

"Can't recall," I said.

Neither could he.

We worked the next week, half days only. It was all the manual labor our poor old bodies could take.

Charlie Rivers gained enough strength to make a brief appearance on Friday. When he saw our progress, he split an apple branch and located number nineteen.

Devaney handed him a reflector to mark the spot. While he stood poking it into the soft soil the crows fluttered back in threes and fours.

"Hoag, Devaney, you guys have been great," Charlie Rivers said. "And I thank you with all my heart. But I know I can handle it from here on. That's nineteen, so there's one left—probably the sentry. My guess is I'll find him in that last corner. I've got two and a half weeks. Weather permitting, I'll make it just fine. I'll get back to clearing brush tomorrow. Thanks again."

We were pretty tuckered out, so being dismissed didn't feel so bad. We told him we did have stuff to do in our own lives, but we'd check in on him regularly, see if he needed anything. We shook hands, packed up our tools, and left.

It rained ten of the next fourteen days. The whole Upper Valley was one gigantic puddle. The French Acre wasn't immune. Several times when it was coming down hard, we drove by and saw Charlie Rivers sipping coffee in his pickup truck, parked in front of the nine-foot wall, waiting for the rain to slack off enough so he could wade in and fight to get a little chainsaw work done. He made little progress in the two-week stretch. Even if we had wanted to, there wasn't a thing we could do to help.

Monday and Tuesday, the seventeenth and eighteenth, I was tied up with a couple of writing assignments farther south in Springfield and Ascutney. But I didn't need a photographer, so Devaney helped Charlie out for part of the day.

"The guy's killing himself," Devaney told me on the phone the second night. "He's there at dawn and works until dark. And I don't believe he's fully recovered from that flu yet."

I told Devaney I had to make another trip south Wednesday on the Springfield story, but I'd try to help out Thursday.

"Have you found out why the deadline is the twenty-fourth?" I asked.

"He's pretty tight-lipped about it," Devaney said. "Near as I can figure, it's the day before the full moon, so maybe there's a tie-in there."

Wednesday afternoon when I got home from Springfield I had a message from Nelda Potter on the answering machine.

"He's got the whole place lit up," Nelda told me when I called her back. "He's been working the last two nights there, running a generator and electric lanterns.

I don't drive at night, but my neighbors told me. They said it looks positively eerie, the light shining through the opening in the wall where the boys hit it, and lit up like a searchlight from inside, shining toward the heavens. The crows stay there at night now. I don't think they did that before."

I phoned Devaney, who had just gotten back from helping Rivers at the French Acre.

"I saw the generator and the lanterns, but I didn't realize Charlie had been staying round the clock," Devaney said. "I'm only on days. We're making headway and, if you help out, the three of us should have it all cleared by this weekend—Monday at the latest, and that's the twenty-fourth. Still, I'm betting we'll get it done and he'll locate the last grave by the weekend."

Thursday morning Devaney picked me up and we drove to the French Acre. Charlie's pickup was parked in front, but when we stepped through the opening in the wall, he wasn't anywhere to be seen. The generator wasn't running and there were no lanterns lit. The area of uncleared brush was down to about thirty-by-thirty. We stepped back out toward the road and looked in the pickup. Charlie was stretched across the bench seat, curled up under an Army blanket.

"I hope he's just asleep," Devaney said, and prepared to rap on the window.

"Don't," I said, grabbing his wrist. "The man's exhausted. He needs the rest. You and I can get started without him."

We cleared brush as quietly as we could for two hours, not firing up the chainsaw. Finally Charlie Rivers appeared behind us.

"Morning," he said. "Thanks for letting me catch a few winks."

"No problem," I said. "No sense killing yourself over a deadline. Besides, we'll make it by Monday night, no sweat. The weather report for the four or five days is good—*at least until the full moon.*"

Rivers smiled. He knew I was fishing.

"More than a full moon," he said, and turned to walk back out of the Acre. "If you two don't mind, I've got to pick something up at Dan & Whit's. Then I've got to hitch up my trailer and pick up a load. Back in a couple of hours."

Devaney and I worked until noon, then knocked off for the day as planned. Using two chainsaws we had made a commendable dent in what remained. Rivers still hadn't returned by the time we packed up and left.

Carol invited her mother and father over for dinner that night, and after we gave an update on the French Acre, my mother-in-law said, "Is this some kind of a special full moon?"

"Good question, Mom," Carol said. "You mean, like a harvest moon, a corn moon, a wolf moon—one of those superstition things? Wolves howling, asylums and emergency rooms filling up, people freaking out? I read somewhere that lunar and lunatic come from the same Latin word."

Before Devaney could roll his eyes, I said, "You know, could be you're onto something. We like to check out all possibilities, don't we, Devaney?"

He rolled his eyes. "Well, it's not a Blue Moon," he said. "That's when you get a second full moon in the same month—like first and twenty-ninth, second and thirtieth, third and thirty-first. I don't know about the others."

While the three of them were having dessert, I went to my study and got on the Internet, planning to do a search for Full Moon. But Devaney's comment about the Blue Moon had stuck in my mind. I typed Blue Moon in instead of Full Moon. A World Book encyclopedia article came up.

The term blue moon *was used as early as 1528 to represent an absurd belief. Later, people described uncommon events as occurring "once in a blue moon." Blue moon also refers to rare types of full moons.*

Two types of full moons qualify. *According to one definition, a blue moon is the second full moon in a month that has two full moons.* According to an older definition, a blue moon is the third full moon in a season that has four full moons. *The older definition was developed using a calendar in which spring always begins on March 21.*

So a blue moon wasn't simply the second full moon in the same month, as Devaney had said and as I had always thought. There was an older, different definition.

I did a computer search for phases of the moon and came up with charts from the U.S. Naval Observatory. I found the one for the current year, 1996. In the autumn quarter the full moons fell on September 27, October 26, November 25, and December 24—four full moons in a quarter. And the third one—*the blue moon*—would be on Tuesday, November 25 at 4:10 a.m. It was the definition I hadn't known about, the one that didn't require two full moons in the same month. Charlie had said it was more than just a full moon.

So that was why Charlie Rivers needed to be done by Monday night, the twenty-fourth. Although the date of the blue moon would be Tuesday, the twenty-fifth, because it was in the wee hours of the morning Tuesday, it would seem as if it were appearing late Monday night, after midnight.

I printed out a copy of the article and the astronomical chart to show Devaney. Retired history teachers could be such know-it-alls, but they weren't always right.

"Maybe he figured there was going to be an even worse accident on the blue moon," Devaney said. "So he wanted to clear and mark all the graves with the flags. You know, the honorable thing, thinking it'd set things right and save some lives."

"Sounds plausible," I said. "But who can say? I sure don't know what's in that man's mind. As he said, we'll have to wait and see."

Friday morning we were met by more than a hundred bales of straw stacked at the opening in the wall. Charlie's pickup and utility trailer weren't around, but there was a note pinned on a bale of straw blocking the opening: *Devaney and Hoag. Can you move the straw inside? Don't break the bales apart, just space them evenly around the ground. Back soon. Thanks. C.T.R.*

"Looks like we're going to seed it and cover it with straw for the winter," Devaney said. "We'll have grass in the spring. Old Charlie's gonna give the town a park."

We had lugged the last bales inside and were resting on them when the pickup and trailer pulled up in front and Charlie beeped his horn. Devaney and I clambered out to see what he wanted.

The truck and trailer were piled high with more bales. The three of us unloaded them and, under the watchful eyes of the crows, hauled them inside the compound.

By Sunday noon we had all the brush and trees cut, cleared, and piled outside the walls. It took Charlie less than five minutes to locate the twentieth soldier's resting place. I marked it with a reflector.

"That's all of them, right, Charlie?" Devaney said.

"Twenty. That's it. But just to be sure, I'll make a

final sweep of the place after lunch. That'll be it, guys. Your work is done. I appreciate all the time and labor you've put in."

"But what about the straw?" I said.

"Yeah. Where's the grass seed?" Devaney added. "Don't you want us to help you seed it?"

Charlie stared at us. "Oh, the seed? Umm, I haven't picked it up yet. I'll get it tomorrow—and I'll rent a spreader—it'll be light work. I can handle it myself. Can't spread the straw until the seed's laid down, but the straw will be light work, too. You two have done more than enough. Thanks."

"But I thought you had a deadline of tomorrow?" Devaney said.

"And what about the flags?" I said.

Charlie Rivers looked sheepish.

"Charlie, you didn't bust your hump to clear this place out by tomorrow just to create a town park. It's about them," I said, motioning around us at the reflectors, "the soldiers."

"Yeah, Charlie," Devaney said. "Why don't you spill it?"

Rivers looked uncertain for a moment, measuring us. Then he said, "Tomorrow night. Come after midnight, right around three-thirty in the morning. Nobody else. Just you two. I'll take care of everything between now and then. Don't come beyond the opening in the wall, though. Stay outside."

"Okay," I said. "Three-thirty, not before. Just the two of us. Can you tell us what you're going to do?"

"No, I can't," Rivers said. "And Hoag, Devaney, promise me—no cameras. Promise. No cameras."

"Promise," I said, Devaney standing dumbly beside me.

The rest of that day and all of Monday we honored Charlie's request and left him alone. Twice on Monday we drove by and saw his vehicle there. On our first pass we noticed he'd picked up another load of straw, which he carried in without help. On the second pass we saw him carrying ropes and two-by-fours. But we didn't stop.

Devaney came by after supper and we half-watched a couple of TV shows. Our minds weren't on TV, they were on Charlie Rivers and the French Acre. We rehashed all the information we'd collected, went over everything we'd seen and done. But, except for the idea of a memorial service, we had no idea.

"He said no cameras," Devaney said. "But he didn't say no tape recorders."

"I've got two in my coat," I said. "One in each pocket." We each had heavy winter coats, scarves, gloves, and hats. It was going to be a very cold, frosty night, the forecast said, but no wind chill.

We watched the ten o'clock news on one channel, the eleven o'clock news on another, and a late-night talk show. When we couldn't stand it any longer, we went out to an all-night truck stop for bacon and eggs. At 2 a.m. we paid the bill, walked out into the parking lot under what seemed to be a full moon and slowly made our way toward the French Acre.

We rounded the last curve onto the straightaway and could see it. With the light of a full moon above and lantern light inside, it looked eerie, like a huge crown that was glowing on top. It wasn't yet 2:30, so we pulled off the road two hundred yards before it. Devaney pulled out the thermos he'd filled at the truck stop and we drank a couple more cups of coffee. We saw Charlie make a couple of trips to the truck, the last one for a ladder.

I heard Devaney's door open.

"Just got to step out and pee," he said. "Get rid of some of this diner coffee."

When I looked out his window a minute later, I saw a camera in front of his nose. I pressed the button and lowered his window.

"What are you doing?" I said. "I thought you were peeing. We promised Charlie no cameras."

Devaney clicked off a shot, turned his head toward the open window, and whispered loudly, "I *am* peeing. A good photographer has to be able to do two things at once. And I heard Charlie to say he wanted no cameras *inside*. And, regarding no cameras, I believe he said *after* three-thirty."

Sometimes Devaney could split hairs and mince words better than the teenagers he'd taught. This wasn't the time to argue with him.

"Hurry up," I said. "The cold air's pouring in."

He climbed back in and closed the door as quietly as he could. I hoped Charlie hadn't heard the noise or caught a glimpse of our dome light while the door was open.

"So what've you got besides the camera?" I said. "Video surveillance equipment?"

"As a matter of fact, I've got the mini-video cam in the bag behind me, and a collapsible tripod. I know we can't take it inside, but I figured we could set it up just before 3:30 outside the hole in the wall. It's the only way I'll get any shots to compare with the others I took." Devaney had shot dozens of rolls of film the past several months, both inside and outside the French Acre. The walls of his study bore witness to the gradual success of Charlie's brush-clearing efforts.

At a quarter-past-three I started the engine and we eased behind Charlie's utility trailer. The light shining in the French Acre silhouetted the hundreds—maybe thousands—of crows on the wall. We could see the moonlight shining off the feathers of the ones closest to us. They seemed to glow an iridescent blue-black, as if they had auras.

Devaney opened his door and started to climb out.

"Hey, what are you doing?" I said, putting a hand on his arm. "It's early."

"Relax," Devaney said. "I'm simply going to see if everything's okay with Charlie. Maybe he needs a little last-minute help." Then he added, "Besides, I figured I'd get set up." He reached for the mini-cam on the back seat.

"Just wait," I said. "Give him until twenty-five after, anyway."

Devaney gave me a pouty look and reluctantly slid back into the car. I pulled out my two miniature tape recorders and tried them. Both worked fine.

"A little nervous?" Devaney said. "Eager to get down to brass tacks?"

Before I could answer, a truck pulled up behind us. I sighted along my outside mirror and saw a large figure in heavy clothing get out. He walked straight toward my driver's-side window. He approached like a cop on a traffic stop.

"Hoag? Devaney?" a deep voice said as I lowered my window. I tried to look up at the man, but he shone a flashlight right in my eyes. "You're both under arrest," he said, then started to giggle, "for idiocy!"

"Dutch? Dutch Roberts?" I sputtered. Well, what the—?"

Both Dutch and Devaney were laughing now.

"Devaney," I said. "Did you tell him we'd be here tonight?"

"Yes, he did," Dutch said. "He called me during *The Tonight Show.*"

"Hoag, I know nothing's going to happen," Devaney said. "But we could be walking into an ambush, and nobody else knows we're here."

"Ambush? You think Charlie's taken almost three months to set us up for an ambush? What's he going to do—scare us to death?"

The two of them kept chuckling.

"All right, Dutch, get in the back seat, damn it. But first," I said, catching a glimpse of the holster on his hip, something he almost never wore, "please put that pistol in your glove compartment. There's nobody here but me, Devaney, a sick old Indian dowser, and a boat-load of crows."

Dutch obliged.

When it was time, we all got out and approached the wall.

"Look at that," Devaney said. "He must have seed-ed it all by himself."

Dozens of kerosene lanterns hung from spikes pounded into the inside walls. Every inch of ground had been covered with loose straw. But the layer of straw was far too thick to be protecting newly sown grass seed. The straw looked to be more than a foot deep. The driveway reflectors were gone. In their places were small British flags taped to the ends of long, straight branches.

"What in the hell is that?" Dutch said, pointing toward the center of the French Acre.

Something like a tree fort, a cross between a duck blind and a giant rattan barstool, stood eight feet above the ground on poles. The wooden ladder we'd seen ear-lier was leaned up against it.

Charlie Rivers sat cross-legged in its center, head down, forearms on knees, palms upturned.

"What's he doing?" Devaney whispered. "Yoga?"

"Some kind of meditation," Dutch said.

Devaney set up his tripod and mounted the mini-cam on it. He panned across the Acre a couple of times, wanting to capture the bluish-gold color of the straw, which looked like an ocean. He zoomed in on Charlie in the tower, then panned around at the faces of the crows, every one facing the tower.

"Has he got his eyes closed?" Dutch said.

"Of course he does," Devaney said. "He's meditating."

A moment later Charlie Rivers began removing his clothing.

"It's ten minutes before four o'clock," I said into the tape recorder. "After a period of what appears to have been meditation, the man we're watching has started taking off his protective clothing. Hat, coat, boots, shirt."

"Damn, he's got to be freezing," Dutch said. "Is this a man in his right mind?"

Charlie's striptease went on for ten minutes as if it were a ritual thing until he had nothing left but his long underwear and tee shirt. At four o'clock I reported into my tape recorder that he was sitting bucknaked on the platform.

"Oh-ah-wa-hay-ye-ah," Charlie chanted. The tape player was too far away to pick it up, but I repeated into it what I thought I heard Charlie saying. He sang it like a mantra, kept repeating it the way I'd heard Native American rain dancers do it in Arizona.

A cloud passed across the moon and I felt a chill run down my spine. It was 4:05 when I mentioned the cloud and my chill on the tape.

"It's some kind of purification ceremony, ain't it?" Dutch said.

Neither Devaney nor I answered.

Rivers had lit six lanterns and arranged them on the platform around him. He prepared what looked like a smudge pot on his lap and began streaking his face. At first I thought of war paint. Then I thought of

Ash Wednesday, the first day of Lent, and my mind conjured up a memory of my wife Carol returning from the worship service at church with a smudge of ash on her forehead, a sign of repentance.

"What time is it, Dutch?" Devaney said.

"Four-oh-nine," Dutch said, and before he could say more the crows moved—just slightly, ever so slightly—all of them. We heard their feathers rustle, all of their feathers together.

"Jeezus," Devaney said, and we all shivered. "What was that about?"

"Four-oh-nine, as I said," Dutch answered. "Four-oh-nine and going on the witching hour."

Charlie stood up on the platform with his arms raised, with what appeared to be leather thongs around his biceps. He continued chanting to the skies, maybe to the gods. Or was it to the moon? *To the blue moon?*

We saw the crows move again, heard the sea of feathers rustle.

"What happens now?" Dutch said.

"I don't know," I said. "Four-ten. Full moon. Wait and see."

Charlie stopped chanting. He turned around in a circle once, twice, three times, and reached for the lanterns. He swung in a softball pitcher's windup and flung them toward the corners of the compound. One. Two. Three. Four. Five. Six. The lanterns landed, some without breaking, others with the sound of shattering glass chimneys. The loose straw quickly caught fire around each lantern.

"Rivers!" Dutch yelled. "What in hell are you doing? You goddamned fool, get out of there." He sprang through the opening but immediately floundered in the loose straw and fell over.

"Dutch, get back here," Devaney screamed. "You can't get to him now."

The two of us grabbed the constable and dragged him back to the opening.

Charlie stood chanting wildly. In no time the entire surface of the compound was engulfed in flames. The crows stood their ground, moving their wings in wider sweeps now—*fanning the flames*—bringing in oxygen from outside the wall. They cawed, a cacophony that mixed with but didn't drown out Charlie Rivers' insane chanting. The six separate fires from the lanterns connected and moved toward the center, bound for Charlie's tower. We saw the twenty British flags disappear in the hungry flames.

"Oh my God, oh my God," we would later hear Devaney say on tape.

A moment later the heat was so intense we had to back away from the opening. Even above the snapping and popping, though, we heard the tower come crashing to the ground, and Charlie's screams.

The crows lifted off *en masse* then as Devaney and I stood transfixed, watching stupidly as they flew across the moon and out over the deep dark woods.

Dutch ran to his truck to call the Fire and Police Departments. By the time they arrived the French Acre was nothing but a smoking black smudge. The only flames they could douse came from the support poles of Charlie's tower.

Devaney and I sat weeping while the Town and State Police asked us questions.

It was days before we could bear to check the audiotapes and mini-cam footage. We were pretty sure we knew everything we had said on the audiotape. But right after we pulled Dutch up from his fall into the soft straw, as Devaney was saying, "Oh, my God. Oh, my God," we could hear Dutch say, "See them? Soldiers. Blue smoke soldiers." With the intensity of the moment, and with Devaney saying, "Oh, my God.

Oh, my God," neither of us recalled Dutch uttering that. And upon questioning, Dutch said he couldn't remember saying it, either. Nor did he remember seeing it. Even when we played the tape, he swore it made no sense to him. Nothing, no blue smoke soldiers—nothing at all—showed up on the videotape to corroborate it.

"So what do you think it was all about?" Devaney said as we tried to piece it all together in my study. "What'll you put in the story?"

Another *Valley News* staffer had already written up the basic fire story—I was too caught up in it—but there was space reserved in the weekend supplement for the special report I'd be delivering.

"Well, we can tell Charlie's side of it," I said. "We can clear up the misconception that it's Lafeyette's French soldiers, explain about Norwich, Connecticut. It'll be interesting to bring in Charlie's background—Abenaki, cemetery groundskeeper, funeral parlor assistant, dowser. We've got the part about the British flags bought at Dan & Whit's, the decades of automobile fatalities, your time and my time working with Charlie. What we saw the night of the blue moon. The crows. Everybody on the road had been talking about the crows. There's plenty here for a story."

"I know that, Hoag. I know there's plenty. But what was it all about? Was it a purification ceremony? Give the soldiers a funeral with honor?"

"Well, sure, obviously it had to be some of that," I said. "But—"

"But what?"

"My guess is, Charlie Rivers didn't tell it all to me, because if he did, he'd have tipped me off that he was going to die in the process, and he knew I'd try to stop him. You see, he told me those Colonial women obtained a sleeping potion they mixed in with the food they fed the soldiers. Charlie didn't say a drug, he said a *potion*. Remember how he used the same word—*potion*—when we took the chicken soup to him? The word *potion* suggests to me it's a pass-down story, handed from generation to generation of Abenaki medicine men and medicine women. That's how his mother got it. He said she was a medicine woman. A potion is something you get from an herbalist, a naturopathic specialist who knows natural cures and remedies—*a medicine woman.*"

"You mean a long-lost, distant relative of Charlie Rivers?" Devaney said.

"Maybe. But it probably doesn't matter if it was a blood relative or not. It's an issue of honor for the entire tribe."

"Is that what the accidents were about?" Devaney said. "Remember how the victims all had Abenaki roots? Was the French Acre calling for Abenaki blood?"

"Charlie may have recognized that all along. But it wasn't until the wall opened up after the last accident that he *sensed* it in his unique way, when he went past the scene the morning after."

"You think Charlie felt it was his duty to do penance, to atone for his tribe's sin?"

"Sin's more a Judaeo-Christian word," I said. "I think Charlie's people would say *dishonor.*"

"But it was the colonial women who slit the throats of those soldiers," Devaney said.

"True," I said. "But it was Charlie's Abenaki ancestor, the medicine woman, who supplied the potion. So, whether she knew how the sleeping potion would be used or not, she had a hand in the murder of twenty men."

"But why did the act of atonement—this making right—have to coincide with the blue moon?" Devaney said.

"I'm not sure," I said. "Maybe if we ask an Abenaki medicine person, we'll learn the answer to that. Or maybe it was just something Charlie sensed—you know, with that sixth sense he had. Maybe he just knew that's when it would work."

"What do you mean—work?" Devaney said.

"Apparently the ceremony, Charlie's sacrifice, worked. I think that's what Dutch—or somebody, *maybe Charlie through Dutch*—was telling us on the tape. *Blue smoke soldiers? Blue* smoke, *blue* moon? Think it's a stretch?"

"I don't know, Hoag" Devaney said, shaking his head. "Maybe. It's a theory. Good thing is, the mystery's solved."

The following spring a team of forensic anthropologists unearthed the remains of twenty men. Buttons and other evidence indicated they had been British soldiers who died during the Revolution. Attempts to determine causes of death were inconclusive. The remains were returned to England.

Two years later the Town dismantled the wall and built a Little League field on the French Acre. Now, for the first time in two hundred years, the French Acre teems with life. The park has been aptly named Soldiers Field.

O R D E R   F O R M

Burt Creations

PLEASE SEND ME THE FOLLOWING:

QUAN.	ITEM	PRICE
_____	**A Christmas Dozen** Hard Cover Book ($17.95)	_____
_____	**A Christmas Dozen** Paperback Book ($14.95)	_____
_____	**A Christmas Dozen** Double cassette ($15.95)	_____
_____	**A Christmas Dozen** Double CD ($16.95)	_____
_____	**Unk's Fiddle** Paperback ($13.95)	_____
_____	**Odd Lot** Paperback Book ($14.95)	_____
_____	**Even Odder** Paperback Book ($14.95)	_____
_____	**Oddest Yet** Paperback Book ($14.95)	_____
_____	**Wicked Odd** Paperback Book ($14.95)	_____
_____	**Odd/Even/Oddest/Wicked** Four Pack ($54.80)	_____

Shipping & handling is $4.50 first item, $2.50 per additional item. Connecticut residents add 6% sales tax.

SALES TAX _____

SHIPPING _____

TOTAL _____

FREE SHIPPING ON ORDERS OF MORE THAN 10 UNITS

NAME _____

ADDRESS _____

CITY _____ STATE _____ ZIP _____

TELEPHONE _____ FAX _____ EMAIL _____

PAYMENT:

❑ Checks payable to: **Burt Creations**
Mail to: 29 Arnold Place, Norwich, CT 06360

❑ VISA ❑ MasterCard

Cardnumber:_____
Name on card:_____
Exp. Date: _____(mo) _____(year)

■ **Toll free order phone** 1-866-MyDozen (866-693-6936 / Secure message machine) Give mailing/shipping address, telephone number, MC/Visa name & card number plus expiration date.
■ **Secure Fax orders:** 860-889-4068. Fill out this form & fax.
■ **On-line orders:** www.burtcreations.com
order@burtcreations.com

www.burtcreations.com